THE MAN OF BRONZE

Raised from the cradle for his task in life, Clark Savage, Jr., goes from one end of the world to another, righting wrongs, helping the oppressed, liberating the innocent.

With limitless wealth at his command, Doc has the best of scientific equipment and supplies. He maintains his New York headquarters as a central point, but in addition has his Fortress of Solitude at a place unknown to anyone, where he goes at periodic intervals to increase his knowledge and concentrate.

His "college" in upper New York is a scientific institution to which he sends all captured crooks, for there, through expert treatment, they are made to forget all of their past and start life anew.

Bantam Books by Kenneth Robeson
Ask your bookseller for the books you have missed

#1   MAN OF BRONZE
#2   THE THOUSAND-HEADED MAN
#8   THE LAND OF TERROR
#9   THE MYSTIC MULLAH
#10 THE PHANTOM CITY
#11 FEAR CAY
#12 QUEST OF QUI
#13 LAND OF ALWAYS-NIGHT
#14 THE FANTASTIC ISLAND
#80 THE KING MAKER
#81 THE STONE MAN
#82 THE EVIL GNOME
#83 THE RED TERRORS
#84 THE MOUNTAIN MONSTER
#85 THE BOSS OF TERROR
#86 THE ANGRY GHOST
#87 THE SPOTTED MEN
#88 THE ROAR DEVIL

About Doc Savage:

DOC SAVAGE: HIS APOCALYPTIC LIFE
by Philip José Farmer

THE ROAR DEVIL

A Doc Savage® Adventure

KENNETH ROBESON

BANTAM BOOKS · TORONTO · NEW YORK · LONDON

*This low-priced Bantam Book
has been completely reset in a type face
designed for easy reading, and was printed
from new plates. It contains the complete
text of the original hard-cover edition.*
NOT ONE WORD HAS BEEN OMITTED.

THE ROAR DEVIL
*A Bantam Book / published by arrangement with
The Condé Nast Publications Inc.*

PRINTING HISTORY
Originally published in DOC SAVAGE *Magazine June 1935*
Bantam edition / May 1977

All rights reserved.
Copyright 1935 by Street & Smith Publications, Inc.
Copyright © renewed 1963 by The Condé Nast Publications Inc.
*This book may not be reproduced in whole or in part, by
mimeograph or any other means, without permission.*
*For information address: The Condé Nast Publications Inc.,
350 Madison Avenue, New York, N.Y. 10017.*

ISBN 0–553–02636–4

Published simultaneously in the United States and Canada

Bantam Books are published by Bantam Books, Inc. Its trade-
mark, consisting of the words "Bantam Books" and the por-
trayal of a bantam, is registered in the United States Patent
Office and in other countries. Marca Registrada. Bantam
Books, Inc., 666 Fifth Avenue, New York, New York 10019.

Contents

I	The Devil in the Woods	1
II	Calamity	8
III	The Bronze Man	16
IV	The Peril Puzzle	23
V	Renny and the Siren	31
VI	A Night for Trading	40
VII	Waterloo for Two	47
VIII	The Dead Man's Voice	53
IX	The Devils Collide	62
X	Trail	69
XI	His Honor	77
XII	The Wronged Inventor	84
XIII	One by One	94
XIV	Candidates for Death	97
XV	The Break	106
XVI	The Unsuccessful Surrender	112
XVII	Mayor Ricketts	120
XVIII	Rendezvous	129
XIX	Cache	136
XX	Hell in a Rock Box	144

Chapter I

THE DEVIL IN THE WOODS

The flat-faced man looked tough. He also gave the impression of one who had been around a bit. Yet he was deceived by a very simple ruse.

He had been looking into the radiator of the gray car to see how much water there was, and when he straightened, he saw the purse and the wrist watch.

He should have realized they had not been there a moment before. He didn't.

He had been a fighter once. There were mounds of gristle about his eyes, his nose was flat and his ears did not have their original shape. He looked evil, but not stupid.

The flat-faced man rubbed his jaw with the back of his hand, which held a stubby black pistol, then he walked over to the hand bag and the watch and examined them.

The hand bag looked expensive, but it was hard to tell, because the makers of imitations have become skillful. Six diamonds around the wrist watch dial sparkled in the afternoon sun in a manner which could not have been equalled by glass. That was not cheap.

Then the man made his mistake. He pocketed his gun, so as to pick up both bag and watch at once. It was hard to say why he did that. Greed, possibly. He got his hands on the articles.

"Now hold onto them!" directed a woman's voice.

She came out from behind a bush that was thick with new, green spring leaves. She held a light .22-caliber automatic rifle pointed at the flat-faced man.

1

The man made an awful face that he must have practiced back in the days when he was a fighter, to scare opponents in the ring.

"You're the babe what's been followin' us!" he growled. He scowled at the little rifle.

The girl—she was in her early twenties—let him look more directly into the muzzle of the .22.

"The hole where they come out may not look big," she said. "But don't let that fool you. They're the new high-speed cartridges. Hold onto the bag and the watch."

The flat-faced man held onto them.

"You are Stupe Davin," said the girl.

"Never heard of the guy," the man denied promptly.

"Bend over and write it out in the dust of the road with your finger."

"Huh?" The man looked blank.

"I am deaf," said the girl. "Write it out."

The man stooped, used a finger and scratched, "D-o n-o-t k-n-o-w D-a-v-i-n," in the dirt.

"Liar," snapped the girl. "You pretend to be the private secretary of Maurice Zachies, known as the Dove of Peace, or Dove Zachies. Actually, you are his bodyguard and hired killer."

The man scraped, "N-o!" in the road.

The girl now searched him, and found a driver's license made out to Albert W. Davin.

"You are Stupe Davin," she said, and pocketed the license.

The man suddenly abandoned pretense. His flat face went purple with rage.

"The devil with you!" he snarled. "I got your number!"

"Write it!" the girl commanded.

"You're workin' for the Roar Devil!" the man yelled.

The girl stood very still, and there was on her features the slightly blank and inquisitive look of those who do not hear well.

"I cannot hear you," she said. "Write it."

The man only snarled stubbornly.

She poked him with the gun. "Write it!"

He growled, "Listen, babe, I ain't opening my face to no——"

He did not finish, for the girl struck him suddenly and unexpectedly with his own automatic pistol, which she had taken from his pocket. She was tall, athletic, and there was nothing mincing about the way she swung the gun against his temple. The flat-faced man did not move after he fell.

There was a cheerful recklessness in the girl's manner as she held the fellow's wrist to ascertain that he was only senseless. She seemed to be enjoying herself hugely, as if it were only a game. She dragged the man over and dumped him into a thick brush clump.

"And you are Dove Zachies's number one killer," she sniffed.

A pocket of her khaki hunting jacket yielded a small box which, according to the label, held capsules of a standardized sleeping potion to be sold only upon prescription. She got three capsules down the sense-less man's throat, doing it in a manner which a physician could not have improved upon.

She seemed in a hurry, but took time for a brief examination of the car—the doors, particularly. Their glass was thick and bulletproof. She compared the license numbers with the notation in a small green book, and seemed satisfied.

"Zachies's car," she said aloud.

She struck out through the woods, eying the ground.

It had been a wet spring in this mountain section of New York State, and the vegetation was luxuriant, the earth soft enough to hold footprints.

The girl found tracks before long. They had been made by a man with small feet, and the fellow was evidently not dressed for the woods, because he walked around brush clumps which a man in stout garb would have breasted.

The manner in which the trail meandered

showed something else, too. The fellow was seeking
the high spots, rocks and small hills. He was undoubtedly searching for something.

Once, where he had stumbled and fallen, there
was a print which showed he was carrying a submachine gun. The mark left by the drum magazine
was unmistakable.

The girl was eying the marks when the roaring
sound came.

There must have been some intangible forewarn-
ing before the sound came, for a jaybird in a near-by
tree had a sudden, frightened spasm. The jay
screeched and beat madly among the treetops, as if
evading some nameless and unseen horror. Experts
concede that nature's creatures, birds and animals
and the like, frequently sense dangers which humans
miss, and possibly this accounted for the jay's anima-
tion in the warm spring sunshine.

Then came the roar. It was very faint at incep-
tion, almost inaudible, then it became as a locust
swarm, and the locusts, invisible, expanded to titanic
proportions, so that eardrums ached and heads nearly
split from the clamor.

All through the woods, birds beat above the treetops in frightened haste, and down in the brush,
rabbits, chucks, squirrels and an occasional deer broke
cover.

Of all in the woodland, only the girl seemed to
behave in a normal manner. She stood perfectly still
and looked at the frightened wild life. Then she
lifted hands and touched her ears. Her features were
puzzled.

Then, with wild suddenness, she raced out from
among the trees, sought the center of a clearing and
flung herself prone. She was motionless there. It was
as if she awaited some incredible happening.

But nothing occurred, except that the fantastic
roaring died as mysteriously as it had arisen, leaving
only the uproar of the birds.

The girl waited a long time. When she finally
arose, her features—she was remarkably attractive in

a satisfying way—wore a puzzled expression, as if she had expected something that had not happened, and was disappointed.

She continued following the footprints of the man. It was not long before she saw him.

He was a man small in stature but exceedingly plump, and he had gray hair, a neat gray beard. He wore a gray suit, a gray beret, and the impression was of a rotund little fellow, a peaceful dove of a man.

He held a submachine gun with both hands, and he seemed frightened; puzzled. He drove nervous glances about.

"Dove Zachies!" the girl murmured, and lifted her light rifle.

Her rifle was a costly target weapon, equipped with a mount for a telescope sight. She clipped the telescope in place and drew a deliberate bead on the man with the submachine gun. She held her position for a time, then lowered the gun.

"He must be taken alive," she told herself, almost inaudibly. "That was the order."

The plump gray man, "Dove" Zachies, moved on through the woods, and the girl trailed him, her manner one of infinite caution.

Dove Zachies was obviously familiar with the region, for he made directly for certain vantage points which gave him a view of his surroundings. His object seemed to be to make sure no one was about.

Zachies held a general course to the westward, and shortly came upon a cabin of some size. The cabin windows were open, but the door closed.

Zachies knocked upon the door. There was no answer, and he knocked twice more, then tried the knob. The door was not locked, and he entered, his machine gun alert.

Something less than five minutes later, he popped outdoors. He had received a shock. It showed on his face. He was terrified.

He scuttled into the woods as if terribly afraid of being seen, or being overtaken by some dire calamity.

From her concealment behind bushes, the girl stared after him. Curiosity on her features, but no fear. Suddenly, as if she intended to inspect the cabin, then overtake Dove Zachies, she ran forward. Entering the cabin, she kept the .22 rifle alert.

She came into a large room, with a fireplace at one end, a table in the middle, and on each side a wall of bookshelves. The shelves were laden with plain-looking volumes which bore dry, profound titles. She glanced at the back of one. Its title read:

BOSTANTI'S PAPERS ON THE
ELECTROKINETICS OF
VOLATILIZATION

The girl made a face and glanced at others. They were all heavy scientific tomes, many being merely binders in which scientific pamphlets had been inserted.

The cabin had more than one room. The girl advanced to a door, shoved it open with the muzzle of her rifle, and started to enter.

She jerked into a sort of frozen motionlessness and stared at the living dead man in the room.

Living and at the same time dead, was the only thing which adequately described the man's appearance. He was a comparatively young man—no more than twenty-five—and he was freckled, had somewhat coarse features. He was in khaki trousers and an undershirt, with a rubber apron about his middle.

One end of a rope was tied to one of the young man's ankles. The rope was some fifteen feet long, and the other end was tied to a roof beam. A child with moderately strong fingers could have untied the young man. But he had obviously been there for days. He looked gaunt, starved, pitiful.

He was standing slackly erect. If he saw the competent young woman with the rifle, he gave no sign. He did not even look at her.

"You!" the girl said sharply. "What's the gag?"

The starved-looking young man swayed slowly, erratically. He was like a mechanical robot with some of his cogs and levers out of order. He was trying to turn around, but he fell down.

"It's a good act!" the girl said dryly.

Then her eyes became wide. The young man had fallen on a piece of glass, and it had cut his hand, so that crimson was sheeting slowly over the floor; but he gave no sign of feeling or knowing.

The girl whipped a glance over the room. It had been a laboratory, but its contents had been ravaged. Apparatus was broken. Empty stands and pedestals indicated much of it had been carried off bodily. There were ax marks on some of the tables, in some of the coils of the gutted electrical paraphernalia. Some one had systematically wrecked the place.

The young woman lunged to the starved man, tore off his undershirt and tied it about his cut hand. She felt of his skin. He was almost as cold as the dead. She shuddered, then shook him.

"Snap out of it!" she urged. "Who are you? What's wrong with you?"

He made blubbering sounds that were quite horrible.

She tried again, shaking him and demanding, "What is your connection with Dove Zachies?"

Dove Zachies, in the door where he had appeared so silently that the girl had not heard, said, "I hope that you will let me assure you that he has no connection whatever."

Chapter II

CALAMITY

The girl had laid her rifle on the floor. She reached for it instinctively, then withdrew her hands when she saw the submachine gun Zachies had trained upon her.

Zachies looked even more peaceful and dovelike at close range.

"I started back to my car and ran across the tracks you left in trailing me," he told the girl. He had a smooth, cooing manner of delivering his words. "Wasn't I lucky?"

Zachies advanced, put a foot on her gun, grasped the barrel and smashed the light weapon, ruining it. Then he scrutinized the girl curiously.

"I've seen you," he said grimly. "Been trailing me the last few days, ain't you—have you not?" He made the grammatical correction as an afterthought.

The girl shrugged, did not answer.

Zachies grunted, "Working for the Roar Devil, are you not?"

The girl blinked, seemed about to say something, but did not.

"You'll sing plenty before I'm through with you, sister," Zachies told her. "For a long time, I've wanted to get my hands on one of your crowd. You can tell me things. For instance, who is this Roar Devil? How does he manage to accomplish the infernal things he does?"

The girl said nothing. Instead of being afraid,

8

she was bright-eyed with interest. She even smiled slightly.

"A lot of babes would be scared silly," Zachies said dryly. "You're a queer one. But leave it to the Roar Devil to pick the tops. Whoever he is, he is good." Zachies suddenly made a hard fighting jaw queerly at odds with his meekly birdlike exterior. "But not good enough, babe!"

The girl had tucked a small purse into a pocket of her canvas hunting jacket, and Zachies wrenched that out and went through it. There were initials on the outside:

R. M. K.

Inside was a case of cards which bore a name corresponding with the initials. He eyed them.

"Retta Marie Kenn," he said. "Is that your name?"

The girl smiled, "You will have to write it out. I am quite deaf."

"Yes?" The man scowled at her, as if not sure whether she were telling the truth. He shook his hand, and continued going through the purse, keeping, however, a close watch on the girl and on the starved-looking young man who was picketed by the rope.

Zachies came upon the driver's license which had belonged to the burly driver of the car back at the road. He had no trouble fathoming how it had come into her possession.

"So you gathered in Stupe Davin," he said grimly. "I'll kick his flat face off for this!"

The girl smiled nicely at him.

Zachies snarled. Then he went on with his search of her belongings. He came upon a telegram, opened it, and read it with much interest:

MISS RETTA KENN
POWERTOWN N Y

TRAIL ZACHIES AND REPORT EACH MOVE HE MAKES
STOP IF POSSIBLE SEIZE HIM AND DELIVER HIM TO ME
V VENABLE MEAR

"Who the devil is V. Venable Mear?" Dove Zachies yelled.

"Write it out!" the girl pleaded.

Dove Zachies made snarling sounds and tramped the room. He was the kind of a man who could not possibly look dangerous, however, and his present rage gave the impression of a pigeon pouting.

He came to a stop with an arm leveled at the starved young man who seemed gripped by some weird stupor.

"Who is this fellow?" Zachies demanded. "What ails him? What makes the fool stand there with that rope around his leg? Why doesn't he untie himself?"

The girl said, "If you will write it. I have a pencil and paper which I carry for——"

"Ahr-r-r!" Zachies howled. "Shut up!"

Zachies glared at the girl's paper and pencil—he could see them protruding from the upper pocket of her jacket. But he made no effort to write out his queries. Instead, he ripped off stout copper wire from a ruined electrical coil in a corner of the room and used it to tie the girl.

She resented that. She scratched his face, hit him in the eye and managed to kick him once, but he got her tied. Then he made a circuit of the place, looking it over, examining discarded shipping crates, old envelopes, the names on newspaper wrappers. He came back and confronted the strange-acting young man who looked so starved.

"You Flagler D'Aughtell?" he demanded. "Or are you his helper, Mort Collins? You two guys are inventors or something, ain't you?"

The starved young man made a bubbling noise.

Zachies eyed him closely and shuddered.

"There's somethin' sure wrong with you," he muttered.

Zachies found a lean-to addition in the rear, which had served as a kitchen. On a table stood a bucket of water. It had been there for days, judging by the number of insects which had fallen into it. Zachies got a dipperful, sloshed some in the starved young man's face, then tried to make the fellow drink some.

The young man did not seem to know how to drink. When Zachies held his head back and poured water down his throat, it was like pouring water into a hose. The young fellow made no struggle, did not even swallow.

"Are you D'Aughtell?" Zachies questioned again. "Or are you Mort Collins? If you're Collins, where is D'Aughtell?"

But the young man had not revived sufficiently to talk. Indeed, if he had revived at all, it was not perceptible.

Zachies scratched his head. Then a bright idea seemed to come. He leaned close to the strangely afflicted young man.

"Roar Devil!" he bellowed. "Roar Devil!"

The young man moved a little, as if by terrific effort. One of his arms came up slightly. It was as if he were trying to get it protectingly across his face.

"Darned if you don't know something!" Zachies muttered. "But the problem is—how to get it out of you."

He considered, and apparently concluded the girl was a more ready source of information, for he turned upon her.

"Who is this Roar Devil?" he growled.

"Write it out," the girl requested.

Zachies snarled, then wrenched the wires off her wrists and from the pocket of her hunting jacket withdrew the paper and pencil.

He started his writing with a fierce jab of the pencil point at the paper. He started violently, emitted a sharp cry, and peered at his finger tips. They bore a strange brownish stain where the pencil had rested.

Zachies made a hoarse sound. He began to sway. He seemed about to faint.

The girl got up calmly from the floor.

Zachies stared at her. He seemed to be growing weaker and weaker.

He gulped, "You did something——"

"The pencil," the girl said dryly. "It's covered with a chemical mixture you probably never heard of. It won't kill you, it that's any consolation."

Zachies sighed loudly and fell flat on his face.

The girl's ankles were still wired. She freed them without particular haste, then used the same tough copper strands to bind Dove Zachies.

The chemical mixture which had made Zachies senseless when he touched the pencil, apparently did not last long, for the man began to stir feebly before the girl finished tying him, so that she had to hold his limbs. She found an upset tool drawer among the laboratory wreckage and from its litter unearthed a roll of black friction tape.

"Got adenoids?" she asked Zachies, who had opened his eyes.

"Naw!" Zachies was shortsighted enough to growl.

The girl grabbed his head, pinched it between his knees and began draping strips of tape across his lips.

"I once heard of a man dying after they taped his lips shut in a robbery," she said conversationally. "He had adenoids."

With Zachies fastened securely, the girl gave attention to the starved young man who was picketed by the rope. She tried Zachies's trick.

"Roar Devil!" she yelled at the young man.

There was enough reaction to prove conclusively that the name Roar Devil meant something momentous to the young man.

The girl now tried to revive the young man enough to talk. She gave him water, forcing it down his throat, and forced down part of a can of corn which she found in the lean-to kitchen. She got nowhere. To her urging to speak, he only blubbered and mumbled.

The young woman apparently did not trust him to remain picketed by the rope, for she used copper wire on his ankles and, after some hesitancy, tape on his lips.

It became apparent that she was going to leave the cabin. Zachies made whizzing noises through his nose and flounced about. The girl, thinking he had something important to say, pulled part of the tape free of his lips.

"What is it?" she demanded.

"You ain't deaf, after all, are you?" Zachies growled.

"Is that all you wanted to know?" she snapped.

"I got to wondering——"

She jammed the gagging tape back in place. Her rifle was hopeless, she saw upon examination. She picked up the submachine gun of Dove Zachies and balanced it thoughtfully.

"Never do to walk into Powertown with this," she concluded, and discarded it.

She picked up the trick pencil which had been Zachies's Waterloo, using a handkerchief so that her fingers would not come in contact with it, and clipped it back in her pocket. The she left the cabin.

She walked rapidly, and since the sun was hot for this portion of the spring season, she was soon carrying her jacket. She was setting a definite course to the southward, but when a bare knob of a hill appeared off to her left, she angled over to it and used a pair of diminutive binoculars to scrutinize the surrounding country.

It was mountainous terrain—some of the most rugged in the eastern United States. Woodland covered the ridges, leaving few bare spots, but the size of the hills and the sweeping depth of the valleys was almost awe-inspiring.

Directly below, a glittering blue mirror under a line of tremendous cliffs, was a sheet of water. The lake was confined by a towering white concrete dam at the lower end.

Within view from where the girl stood there were portions of two other dams, one of these a structure of tremendous size. This section—hundreds of square miles in area—was the great Powertown Drainage Basin Project.

It consisted of several auxiliary dams and one

main dam of vast size. The purpose of these dams was not only the generating of power, but also as a water supply for New York City. The metropolis had become so vast that the older and smaller reservoirs were inadequate.

The young woman seemed to have stopped to rest as much as for any other reason, and now she went on, setting a crow-flight course as nearly as the brush and the precipitous going permitted. This seemed to be a short-cut across the mountains.

Unexpectedly, she stopped. Her face assumed a queerly set expression.

Then it came, not gradually out of nothingness as it had before, but suddenly, violently, with a whooping moan that sent birds shrieking. It was the roar, fantastic, unearthly, a sound that was like no other. It did not throb, did not travel in waves, and there was no gobbling syncopation of echoes such as might have been set up by an ordinary noise—or if there was, the roaring that was the father of them all drowned out all else.

Then it stopped. Abruptly, like something broken off. And it left behind it a world that did not seem normal.

There was no sound now. Where there had been tumult, there was now profound quiet. The birds wheeled in the sky—and they must have been crying out excitedly. Yet there was no slightest noise audible.

The ordinary silence of the woodland had not fallen. It was more than that. All sound had completely stopped. Then other things happened.

The earth jumped—jumped like a live thing that had been kicked. The girl reeled, flailed her arms trying to keep her balance, then fell. Rocks rolled on the ground like popcorn on the bottom of a pan, only not as violently.

After the first tremor, there were others, but they subsided rapidly in violence. The entire surface of the earth had apparently shifted.

The girl arose from where she had been flung, ran to a tree, eyed it doubtfully, then began to climb.

She was halfway up when, as if an electric switch had been turned on, the world seemed to come alive. Before, there had been utterly no sound. Now there was plenty.

She could hear the scrapings of her own climbing efforts, could hear her own labored breathing. And the birds were making a great uproar. There was something else, too—a distant rumbling. She looked toward the source of that noise.

Below her was the dam which she had viewed earlier. It was collapsing. The central section was already gone. A vast torrent of water poured through. On either side, more of the big concrete wall was rapidly upsetting. The valley below was filling with a writhing monster of water that uprooted trees, toppled along boulders as large as small mansions.

Craning her neck, the girl perceived a house in the path of the flood. Near it was a barn, other outbuildings. A man and a woman, their figures made tiny by distance, ran out of the house and stared up the valley at the wall of water. Then they raced to a small car near by and drove madly for safety, until they were lost to view among trees.

The girl shuddered. It did not look as if the fugitives could escape.

The young woman watched for some time from her vantage point in the tree. She seemed particularly interested in the effect the flood would have when it reached the big reservoir. Would the latter hold?

It held. The young woman waited fully three hours before she became certain.

Then she went on toward Powertown, and when she drew near the small metropolis, she went slowly and furtively, as if extremely desirous of escaping discovery.

Chapter III

THE BRONZE MAN

Powertown was in a nervous sweat, and with reason. It had dawned on the town that fully half of its population was in danger, and that some millions of dollars in property were menaced.

Engineers had originally lain out Powertown so that it was above any normal flood which would result from a disaster to the big dam, which was situated some two miles up the valley. But the engineers had reckoned without the sudden popularity of Powertown.

It had become the rage as a summer and winter resort, due to the attractiveness of the surrounding lakes, and as a result, Powertown had spread down on the floor of the valley until most of the business section was in the path of a flood of any major proportions.

Persons in the streets looked frightened. A good part of the population had fled to the surrounding mountains. Since it appeared that the dam was not in imminent danger of collapse, some of the fugitives were returning.

In the new, resplendent Municipal Office Building, which was another name for city hall, the mayor, the city council and other important citizens were conferring. Their faces were heavy.

"It's terrible," said His Honor, Mayor Leland Ricketts.

"It's damned mysterious," said the head of the council. "The dam that broke this afternoon was supposed to be absolutely safe. The engineers said it was proof even against an earthquake."

"It was no earthquake," snapped Mayor Ricketts.

"But the earth moved," retorted the other. "We all felt it. Didn't the shock break windows all over town?"

The city attorney put in, "What about the two engineers whom the council hired to learn what was causing these weird shocks? This afternoon was not the first shock. What about the two engineers?"

The mayor pounded with his gavel for silence.

"My friends and fellow citizens," he said heavily, "I called this meeting in the face of an emergency and a mystery. You all know there have been previous shocks such as the one this afternoon, although none of the others resulted in as much damage. These shocks began three weeks ago, and have continued almost daily, resulting in landslides which have buried roads, broken water mains, and otherwise proved a menace to the sterling citizens of this city who——"

"This is no time for a political speech," whispered the city attorney. "Get down to brass tacks."

The mayor frowned.

"The city council voted to call in engineers to ascertain what was wrong," he said. "We did so, hiring two very famous geologists. During the past few days, these two geologists have been going around in the mountains with their instruments."

"What did they find out?" some one asked.

"They must have learned something," said the mayor. "We do not know what it is, however."

"Is this a riddle?" queried the city attorney.

"Quiet, please," requested the mayor. "I have called this meeting to inform the city council that something has happened to our two engineers."

"What?" several voices chorused.

"That is what I want to show you," said his honor.

He signaled with a hand, and white-clad hospital internes entered the hall, leading two men who acted as if they were dead, yet alive.

These two men could not walk alone. The internes had to lift each man's foot and advance it with every step. Both men were very pale, and when one's mouth fell open, he seemed unable to close it without assistance from one of the white-clad escort. The masklike rigidity of their features was horrible, and a mutter of wonder went up from the assembled city fathers.

"What ails them?" demanded the city attorney.

"That," said his honor, "is what we would like to know. They haven't been able to find out at our new hospital."

"How long have they been this way?" the city attorney gulped.

"Since yesterday. They were found wandering in the mountains."

There was much buzzing conversation, and a crowd gathered about the two weirdly afflicted engineers to examine them curiously. Close inspection of the two victims had the effect of giving every one a case of jitters.

The mayor banged order with his gavel.

"None of this must get into the newspapers," he said warningly.

"No publicity, above all things!" emphatically agreed a man who owned the city's two leading hotels. "People will stop coming to Powertown."

"It might be well if they did," snapped the city attorney. "If the big dam breaks, it'll wipe out half the town, including the resort section."

"No, no!" insisted the hotel owner. "There is no danger."

"The devil there isn't!" retorted the other. "You're thinking of your pocketbook, and not of the lives endangered."

"I resent that!" yelled the other.

The mayor's gavel pounded down noisily.

"We are losing sight of our objective!" he bellowed.

"What objective?" demanded the city attorney.

"The solution of the mystery behind this," said his honor. "We know there is something terrible going on. That it is no natural phenomenon, such as earthquakes, we know, because of what happened to our two engineers. They must have stumbled upon something. What it was, we don't know, because they cannot talk. Something horrible has happened to them."

"Have you got a plan, or are you just talking?" asked the city attorney.

"I have a plan," replied the mayor. "We should have thought of it before. There is a man who makes a career of helping other people out of trouble. He is a very remarkable man, from what I hear, and just the fellow we need."

The city attorney frowned, then nodded to himself.

"A very remarkable man whose career is getting others out of jams," he said. "That description suggests a name. But if it is the same fellow I am thinking of, what makes you think he will come up here. That man is big time. He makes kingdoms and things like that. I've read about him in the newspapers."

"What'll it cost?" asked the man who owned the hotels.

"This man does not work for money," said the mayor.

"Now I know we're thinking about the same fellow," observed the city attorney. "Doc Savage."

"Doc Savage is the man," agreed Mayor Leland Ricketts.

There was no great excitement at mention of Doc Savage—perhaps due to the fact that these were all staid businessmen. Several nodded, however, and there was a murmur of conversation.

It seemed that all of them had heard of Doc Savage.

The mayor banged the meeting into parliamentary session, and it was formally decided to appeal to Doc Savage for assistance in solving the mystery of the violent earth convulsions in the vicinity of Powertown, to say nothing of the strange affliction which had overcome the two hired engineers.

His honor, the mayor, agreed upon as being the

most convincing talker in town, was delegated the job of getting in touch with Doc Savage. It was decided to do this by long-distance telephone. But there a hitch occurred.

The weird earth shock had caused breakage of the telephone wires, which were carried, in the modern manner, in a conduit underground. The telephone company advised repairs would soon be completed.

Waiting, the city fathers engaged in more conversation.

"Queer roaring noises have been reported as heard in the mountains near by," said the city attorney. "It is my opinion that these have something to do with the earth convulsions."

"Opinion based on what?" queried his honor.

"On logic," snapped the other. "The roarings are queer. So are the earth shakings, earthquakes, or whatever they are."

"They are not earthquakes," some one pointed out loudly. "Seismographs in other States do not register them. An earthquake would register. These don't."

The conversation was lapsing into a rehashing of the situation, with no new angles being brought out. His honor tried the telephone again, and was informed that an hour or more might elapse before the long-distance wires were repaired. More than one break had been found.

The hospital internes had gone with the two queerly afflicted engineers. Men with urgent business to attend to began drifting out of the hall.

The Municipal Office Building was a large structure, and flanking it at the rear was one of the town's numerous hotels. This hostelry was neither large nor pretentious. There was a courtyard between it and the Municipal Office Building. No one ever frequented this court.

Possibly the deserted court was the reason why a tiny wire, stretching from a hotel window to the roof of the Municipal Office Building, had escaped discovery. However, it was a very fine wire, no larger than a hair.

Shades were drawn over the hotel window into which the wire led. They were thick shades, and it was gloomy in the room. It would have taxed an observer to catch more than a faint glint of light from a telephonic headset as it was removed from a head and deposited on the floor.

The headset, with an amplifier box near by, the wire across the court, and a microphone cleverly concealed inside the municipal building comprised a very modern eavesdropping device.

The secret listener to the conference in the Municipal Office Building now left the hotel room, walked boldly through the hotel lobby and out into the afternoon sunlight.

It was the young woman who had trailed and captured Dove Zachies. She was smiling, unconcerned, as she made her way to the telephone office and tried to get long-distance connections to New York. The wires were still out.

The young woman made her way to a small private garage on the outskirts of Powertown. She entered, locked the door behind her, and opened the rumble seat of the large coupe which the garage held. She brought out boxes and wires, began to hook them together and set them up.

It was a radio telephone set, one in which portability had been sacrificed somewhat for power. She began calling, "Mear, Mear, Mear!" repeatedly, until a thin, dry-sounding voice answered.

"This is V. Venable Mear speaking," the voice said. "I am in New York."

"Retta Kenn reporting," said the young woman. "I have seized Dove Zachies and his usual shadow, Stupe Davin——"

"Why did you not use the telephone?" demanded the somewhat creaking voice of V. Venable Mear.

"Wires out," said the girl. "I left Zachies bound securely and gagged at the cabin of a man named Flagler D'Aughtell, along with a man who seems to be Mort Collins, the assistant of D'Aughtell. Stupe Davin I left in the heavy bushes by the road near the cabin——"

"What was Dove Zachies doing at D'Aughtell's cabin?" V. Venable Mear demanded sharply.

"Looking" said the girl. "Just looking around, as far as I could tell."

"We will take care of this Zachies matter later," advised Mear. "What else have you learned?"

"I just tuned in on the city fathers," reported the young woman. "They are puzzled and worried."

"That is not news," snorted Mear.

"But this is," informed Retta Kenn. "They are going to call on Doc Savage to solve the mystery."

"What!" exploded V. Venable Mear. "Are you sure?"

"Positively," replied the young woman. "The telephone wires are down now, but as soon as they are repaired, Doc Savage will be started on the trail of the Roar Devil and all of the rest of it."

"Oh, oh!" gasped V. Venable Mear.

"You said it," Retta Kenn agreed. "When the bronze man——"

"Who?"

"The bronze man," exclaimed the girl. "They call Doc Savage that. When he tackles this, things are going to happen."

"Yes," V. Venable Mear agreed, "the Doc Savage angle is something new."

Chapter IV

THE PERIL PUZZLE

Doc Savage was in his office-laboratory on the eighty-sixth floor of a mid-town New York City skyscraper.

The bronze man was attired in an all-enveloping garment of gray rubberized fabric, and his head was encased in what resembled a diver's helmet made of glass. Clad in this hermetically sealed outfit, he was manipulating retorts and stills in which chemicals boiled and precipitated, and from which clouds of evil-looking vapor arose. The laboratory door was closed tightly and locked.

A buzzer whined a loud, shrill note. The bronze man ignored it. The vapor from his chemicals had settled over his glass hood, and occasionally he paused to wipe it away to permit clearer vision. At such times, his features were distinguishable.

Several things were noteworthy about his visage. His skin was fine-textured and of a somewhat unique bronze hue. His hair, straight and fitting like a metal skullcap, was of a bronze slightly darker than his skin. A woman would have called his face remarkably handsome. A man would have noticed the tremendous sinews in his neck and the smooth muscularity about his jaws.

Most striking of all, perhaps, were his eyes. They were like pools of small gold flakes stirred by an uneasy, tiny wind. They were startling, compelling eyes, and they seemed never at ease.

The buzzer whined again. The bronze man lowered the heat of an electric still, then walked to a large instrument panel and threw a switch. On the panel was a square of frosted glass.

The frosted glass lighted up not unlike a small motion picture screen, showing a view of the corridor in front of the elevators.

Doc Savage studied the screen, which merely showed the reflection of the corridor as carried by an arrangement of mirrors and tubes.

Into the atmosphere of the laboratory there came a queer, exotic sound. It was undulating, not unmusical, and it ran up and down the scale without adhering to any particular tune. It was not a whistle, nor yet was it a vocal noise. A listener might have called it a trilling note, if he thought of any description at all.

It was the sound of Doc Savage, small unconscious thing which he made in moments of mental stress.

There was a man in the corridor. He was on his hands and knees, and now he reached up and, with what seemed infinite difficulty, pressed the buzzer button again.

The man was sagging in a little lake of scarlet. He coughed, and a red spray flew threw his teeth. He was a stocky man, and he was very pale.

Doc Savage left the laboratory hurriedly. But he was careful to lock the door behind him, and once in the library with its thousands of scientific volumes, he turned on a strong electric fan and stood a moment in its blast.

He had been experimenting with poison gases, trying to develop a counter-gas which would render them harmless, and enough of the vapors might cling to recesses of his weird garment to kill one who came close.

Satisfied that the fan blast had removed any lethal wisps, he went on into the reception room with its furnishings of deep leather chairs, massive inlaid table and huge safe.

The corridor door behaved in surprising fashion as he approached it. While he was still ten feet from it, the panel, which bore no trace of a knob or lock, opened. It was actuated by a device which a fairly competent electrician could have explained—an electroscope equipped with contacts and wired to relays and a hidden lock in the door. A bit of radioactive metal which the bronze man carried actuated the device.

The man in the corridor was disclosed. The fellow still crouched on all fours. He looked up. His eyes were unnaturally bright.

Doc Savage made no move to pass through the door. He stood well within the reception room, and his flaked-gold eyes roved. Most of their attention centered on the red pool on the floor. When he spoke, it was with a voice of quiet, controlled power, and his tone showed no emotion whatever. He might have been commenting on the ordinary weather.

"Red ink does not make an altogether convincing substitute for blood," he said.

The effect of that statement on the man on the corridor floor was instant and violent. He jerked back on his haunches. His hand, which had been near his coat, dived under that garment and came out with a blue revolver.

The fellow had skill with guns. His weapon lipped flame and powder noise when hardly clear of his coat. He came erect shooting with quick precision. His gun was a type which held five cartridges. He fired four of them. Then he stopped. His eyes seemed about to pop out of his head.

Doc Savage had not moved, nor showed any such surprise as might have been expected. Nor had he been harmed.

The bullets had stopped in mid-air in front of him. Three had flattened and bounced to the corridor floor. The fourth hung suspended, and from it radiated a spider web design which showed what had happened. There was a barrier of thick bulletproof plate glass inside the door.

"Hell!" gritted the gunman, and lunged forward as if to find a way around the protective plate.

Comparative gloom of the reception room made

the glass wall almost indistinguishable, but the gun wielder found it with his hands, then lunged upward, hoping to find a space at the top. There was none. He kicked the glass and cursed.

Doc Savage advanced.

The gunman, frightened now, swore, whirled and ran down the corridor.

Doc did not pursue him immediately, but spun back to the large table which stood before the window. The inlaid top of this appeared innocent, but the mosaic pieces were cunning push buttons. He thumbed one of these.

When he whipped back into the corridor—circling the protective barrier of glass in the proper direction—the gunman was not in sight. He had not gone down the stairway, for that was blocked by a metal gate which was kept locked. He must have taken an elevator.

Doc Savage listened. Usually, sighing noises made by the swift-moving cables came from the elevator shafts. But now there was silence.

The bronze man ran down the stairway, let himself through the gate and continued his descent. On each floor, he examined the elevator doors and listened.

Four stories down, he heard a banging from one of the shafts. Some one in a cage was beating at the metal panels of the sliding doors. Even as the bronze man watched, the metal sheet bent, tore loose.

A fist of unbelievable hugeness delivered the panel a few more blows, then grasped the metal and tore it aside. A man crawled out of the elevator cage, which had stopped below center, so that the safety trip prevented the doors being opened.

The man would have weighed in excess of two hundred and fifty pounds, and yet somehow managed to seem gaunt. He had a long face which bore an expression of puritanical gloom. He looked at Doc Savage and seemed sad to the point of tears.

"What's going on?" he demanded in a voice something akin to the rumble of a disturbed bear in his den.

"Gentleman tried to shoot me, Renny," Doc Savage told him quietly. "He fled in an elevator. I pressed the button which cuts the current off all the elevator cages, stopping them, and now I am hunting the car which has the gunman in it."

"Holy cow!" Renny boomed gloomily.

"Renny" was Colonel John Renwick, world-famous engineer, one of Doc Savage's five assistants.

Renny's expression, as he followed Doc Savage down the stairway, was that of a man going to the funeral of his best friend. But it was a peculiar characteristic of Renny's that, the more gloomy he looked, the more pleased he was with events.

Nine floors down, Doc stopped.

"Listen!" he said.

Muffled profanity was coming out of an elevator shaft. It was the voice of the gun wielder.

"Fortunately, the current went off when his cage was between floors," Doc Savage said. "He was trapped."

The sliding doors into the elevator shafts could be opened by a metal hook of a device, one of which was kept in a niche on each floor. Doc Savage got the doors apart. They could look down upon the grating which formed a part of the cage roof.

"Anæsthetic gas," Renny rumbled, and produced from an underarm holster a weapon which resembled an overgrown automatic pistol, fitted with a drum magazine. It was really a machine pistol capable of a tremendous rate of fire, a product of Doc Savage's inventive skill.

The pistol was carried under Renny's left arm, and under the right was a padded case which held extra ammunition drums, painted in various colors. Renny selected one marked with green paint.

"This one has slugs charged with a gas that'll make him unconscious for about half an hour," he boomed grimly.

He aimed at the grilled cage top. The machine pistol made a sound like a gigantic bullfiddle.

Twenty minutes later, they had the stocky would-be killer in the eighty-sixth floor study, and were watching him give signs of returning consciousness.

"Not a thing in his pockets," Renny rumbled. "You say you never saw the guy before, Doc? I know blamed well *I* never saw him. Why should he try to kill you?"

"That," Doc Savage replied, "is what we will try to find out."

The bronze man had brought from the laboratory an apparatus similar in appearance to those employed in hospitals for the administration of anæsthetics. Now, before the gunman entirely regained consciousness, he fitted the face piece upon the fellow's features and tuned various valves on the supply tanks.

Renny had seen the procedure before, and knew what it meant.

"Truth serum," he said.

"Administered in vaporized form," Doc Savage agreed. "The stuff seems to be more dependable, if used in that manner."

The stocky man did not regain consciousness, in the true sense of the word. He merely passed from the influence of the anæsthetic and came under the spell of the serum.

Doc Savage began to put questions. Some of the replies were coherent; others not entirely clear.

"Why did you try to kill me?" Doc demanded.

"Ten grand," the man mumbled. "Half of it in advance."

"Hired," Renny boomed. "And he got a good price, too. Only he didn't get away with it."

"Who hired you?" Doc asked.

"Telephone," the man droned, his true consciousness unaware of what he was doing. "Money—letter—my mail box."

"Who hired you?" Doc persisted.

"Roar Devil, they call him," said the prisoner.

Renny scratched his head with an enormous finger. "This sounds scatterbrained to me."

"Who hired you?" Doc repeated for the third time.

The man mumbled something they could not understand, but finished, "Roar Devil. Nobody knows more about the chief than that."

Again and again, Doc Savage tried to get information from their victim, only to get a repetition of what had been said previously. Later, there were mouthings which surprised and puzzled them.

"Biggest thing—in history," the doped man rambled. "Millions in it—every crook in country—whether they like it or not—police helpless."

"Sounds like a pipe dream," Renny murmured.

When the effects of the serum began to wear off, Doc Savage administered more.

"Got to get Dove Zachies's cache," their subject rambled. "Tie up grifters in New York—make Zachies see reason—Doc Savage—to be stopped."

Renny eyed Doc. "Ever hear of Dove Zachies?"

"Crook," the bronze man replied. "Rumored to be the brains behind a large organization. I've been intending to give him some attention."

Their prisoner seemed to have divulged all he knew, for his continued ramblings were only repetitions. After a time, he came out from under the influence of the drug. He shut up promptly. To their questions, he replied with profanity.

The telephone rang. It was the mayor of Powertown, who had finally gotten connections over the repaired telephone wires.

"We are face to face with a rather fantastic menace," he told Doc Savage, and went on to repeat substantially the facts which had come out in the conclave of the city fathers in the Municipal Office Building.

"We need the assistance of a man of your ability," his honor finished.

"Have you heard any mention of an individual or thing called the Roar Devil in connection with these mysterious earth tremors?" Doc asked.

"No," said the mayor. "But I told you of the roaring sounds. They are very strange."

"You want me to investigate this?" Doc asked.

"Exactly!"

"One of my five associates, Colonel John Renwick, will be in Powertown within a few hours," Doc Savage said.

The mayor murmured, "But it might be better if you came personally——"

"Later," Doc advised. "Colonel Renwick is one of the world's leading engineers. You can depend on him."

The bronze man hung up.

Renny studied Doc gloomily. "How come?"

"You will go to Powertown," Doc told him. "I will remain in New York, at least for a time, to see what turns up on this other matter." He nodded at the stocky man who had tried to kill him.

"You think this fellow tried to kill you to keep you from looking into the mystery at Powertown?" Renny demanded.

"Entirely possible," Doc told him.

Renny made preparations for his departure. In the midst of them he paused and indicated their prisoner, who was now entirely out from under the effects of the truth serum.

"What about this fellow?" Renny asked. "We've got all we can out of him. What'll we do with him?"

"The thing we usually do with crooks," Doc said, "send them upstate."

Renny said, "I'm going to fly up to Powertown."

"Good luck," Doc told him.

Chapter V

RENNY AND THE SIREN

Renny arrived in Powertown in a small, fast plane. He handled the controls himself. The Powertown Municipal Airport was modern and lighted, so that there was no difficulty about landing, although it was well after sundown.

A taxicab took Renny directly to the Municipal Office Building.

Renny seemed to make quite a favorable impression on the assembled leaders of the town. As a matter of fact, he was a commanding figure, and an interesting one. His enormous hands were especially striking. And he could make a speech as effective as the mayor's.

In a businesslike session, Renny was furnished with all the information available. It was not substantially greater than what had been told over the telephone.

The two mysteriously afflicted engineers were brought in on stretchers. Renny examined them. Such things were not his specialty. He was completely baffled.

"This is something for Doc Savage," he said. "My job is to examine those dams and learn whether they are in immediate danger of collapsing. Too, those strange roaring noises interest me."

Renny requested an aërial photographic map of the region about Powertown. Some one went for it. During the wait, there was more conversation.

Because he wanted to think, Renny drew aside,

seated himself in a deep chair, leaned back and fixed
his eyes on the ceiling. Almost at once, he saw something. He did not realize immediately its significance.

At first, he mistook what he had seen for a cobweb with light shining on it. Then he realized it was
far too long and straight for a cobweb. Too, there
were a pair of the tiny threads.

Wires! It was only the artificial lights and Renny's
excellent eyesight which had led to their discovery.
Renny got up and pretended to walk around the
conference hall while he examined the wires. They
led from the huge, ornate chandelier in the center of
the room to a window at the rear.

Renny took up a position near the door and
rapped a table loudly until he had attention.

"Did you know someone is eavesdropping on
you with a dictograph device?" he demanded loudly,
and pointed out the wires.

There was some excitement. In the middle of it,
Renny ducked out, ran around the block and concealed himself behind a parked car. He knew the
wires must run into some building at the rear of the
hall, and if there was an eavesdropper, the individual
would be fairly certain to take flight. Renny did not
have long to wait.

A young woman came out of a small hotel directly back of the Municipal Office Building. She was
in a great hurry. She hastened down the street.

Renny followed her. He did it expertly, for he was
an old hand at this sort of thing. The young woman
headed toward the residential district.

Once, when he drew close to the young woman,
Renny was absolutely certain he heard her laughing
to herself. It was genuine mirth, as if she enjoyed the
whole thing hugely. Renny also got a better idea of
her appearance as she passed under a street light. She
was an athletic young woman, rather more than ordinarily attractive. Her frock looked expensive, and she
affected a close masculine cut of her dark hair.

Renny's quarry entered a small frame garage near
the outskirts of the town. Loitering outside, he could

hear her voice murmuring, but could not catch the words.

The young woman came out of the garage so unexpectedly that she nearly caught Renny napping. He barely got behind a bush, where the shadows were thick. She walked off rapidly.

Renny ran to the garage door. It was padlocked. He waited a little—until the girl's footsteps died down the street. Then he took the padlock in both his big hands and did something which would have amazed an onlooker. He wrenched the lock off, hasp and all, using only the strength of his huge hands. Fortunately, the screws holding the lock had not been too large.

Inside the garage, Renny found a coupe. In the rumble seat compartment of this was a portable radio transmitter-and-receiver. The tubes were still quite hot.

By a combination of good luck and fast running, Renny managed to overhaul the young woman. He slackened his pace the instant he caught sight of her ahead, and trailed her.

The mysterious young woman headed directly into the mountains. The rugged country around Powertown had never been suited to cultivation, so it was almost entirely woodland. The girl was evidently using a compass, the dial of which she occasionally illuminated with a flashlight.

An hour later, Renny could see the great, moon-brightened mirror of Powertown's enormous main reservoir off to the left, and the young woman ahead was going as strongly as ever. She was following a ridge.

They passed the site of the dam which had burst the previous afternoon. On the floor of the valley, occasional lights moved. These were undoubtedly searching parties in quest of flood victims.

The moon disappeared and a haze obscured the stars, resulting in rather intense darkness. Renny experienced no little difficulty in trailing the girl silently.

The young woman came finally to a little-used mountain road. At the side of this stood a gray sedan. She walked boldly into bushes near by, and seemed surprised at not finding something there.

She drew a small automatic from her frock and became more alert. Renny got close enough to hear her when she spoke disgustedly to herself.

"So!" she snapped. "Some one found Stupe Davin and moved him."

She used her flashlight cautiously, apparently looking for footprints.

"He was moved, all right," she announced to herself. "He would be still asleep from that drug I gave him."

She sounded rather cheerful about it, as if some one had just scored against her in a pleasantly exciting game.

She left the car and continued on through the thick, rugged woodland.

Renny first saw the cabin when it sprang out, a darksome sepulchre of logs, in the glow of the girl's flashlight. She must have stood still for some time and listened, for she had halted, and Renny had halted also, and had waited so long that he had feared he had lost his quarry.

The girl entered the cabin boldly. Renny darted forward. He could manage great silence for one of his bulk. He watched the girl through grimy windows. She roved her flashlight beam, as if looking for something or some one, and entered the room which had been a laboratory.

Renny promptly scuttled into the outer room. He lifted several books and stood them on end across the floor. Then he took up a position to one side.

In the other room, the girl said disgustedly, "It looks as if I did an afternoon's work for nothing."

Then she came back through the door. She did not cast the flash beam on the floor. Her foot hit the first book. It upset, hit the next book, and the whole string of them toppled over with a pattering sound.

Startled, the girl leaped backward. Renny was

moving forward on his toes. His long arms gathered her in. His big right hand clamped over her gun.

She surprised him. He had fought men, more times than he could remember. Few of them had equalled this girl. She must have been an avid exponent of physical culture. She knew something of jujitsu, too. She kicked him and hit him with terrific force. They were both on the floor before Renny got the gun, and that was something he would never brag about, because he considered his own strength by no means ordinary.

"Holy cow!" Renny puffed, and got to his feet. "Talk about your wildcats!"

The girl was up like a shot and nearly demonstrated she could outrun him. He caught her fifty yards from the cabin. She knocked him down once, beautifully, something he would have sworn no woman could do. He got her down on her face and held her there, a big hand pinned against the back of her neck.

"What'd you come up here looking for?" he demanded. "Why were you eavesdropping on that meeting in Powertown?"

"Nuts to you!" said the feminine fire-eater.

"We'll go back to the cabin," Renny said. "We got lots to talk about."

The trip back to the cabin was one he did not soon forget. He tied her wrists with his handkerchief. She broke the bonds and gave him a marvelous black eye. It ended by his grabbing her hair with one big hand and holding her out as far as he could and marching her along. Even then, she managed to kick much of the hide off his shins.

"What a woman!" he said, not without admiration, as they entered the cabin. "I didn't think they came like you."

Three men came out of the darkness within the cabin and pointed guns at Renny and the girl.

Renny was no fool. He rumbled savagely, released the girl and lifted his arms.

"You big tramp!" said the girl, and aimed a swing

at his good eye. He ducked, took the blow on the forehead and looked stunned.

"Cut, Miss Kenn," said one of the gunmen. "We'll handle him now."

The girl glared at them.

"I don't know you!" she snapped.

"You're Retta Kenn, are you not?" asked the spokesman of the gun-holding trio.

"Yes." She scowled. "But I never saw you before."

The other shrugged. "Such is fame."

The girl planted small fists on her hips. She was very mad, but she seemed to be enjoying herself, regardless.

"What comes next?" she demanded.

"You can go back to Powertown and continue your good work," she was informed.

She seemed surprised. "Just who are you, anyway?"

"Friends of yours," grunted the other. "Ain't you wise to that, yet?"

Retta Kenn gasped, "You mean you work for——"

"Eh-heh!" The man held up a warning finger. "No names, sweetness. You just skip back to Powertown. We'll handle the rest of this. You've done a good night's work."

The girl looked very puzzled. Then she left the cabin.

"Follow her," the spokesman ordered one of his men. "See that nobody bothers her, and that she gets back to Powertown."

The men sidled out furtively after the pugilistic young woman.

Renny was searched—and relieved of his machine pistol, the drums of cartridges, a heavy-bladed pocket knife, and somewhat over a thousand dollars in currency which he had brought along for expense money.

"You guys in Doc Savage's crowd really carry pocket change, don't you?" queried the spokesman.

Renny studied the fellow. He was confident he had never seen the individual before. The fellow was lean, neatly dressed and smoothly shaven. His nails were manicured. He wore neat, metal-rimmed spectacles. He looked like a conservative businessman.

"Are we supposed to be acquainted?" Renny demanded.

The other made a gesture of throwing things off his shoulders.

"Indirectly, perhaps," he said. "If we consider acquaintanceship in the category of the tangible and the certain march of circumstances, rather than a concrete expression of——"

"You sound like a guy I know," Renny growled. "Nobody understands him when he talks."

"You mean the estimable William Harper Littlejohn, better known as Johnny?" queried the other. "To tell the truth, we rather expected Doc Savage instead of you. Johnny is the geologist, you know."

"So your crowd sent that guy to shoot Doc in New York?" Renny hazarded.

The neatly clad man smiled and adjusted his spectacles. He did not answer the question directly.

"By the way, what became of the, ah—messenger of death?" he queried.

Renny looked very gloomy. "You won't see him again."

Then something happened which caused Renny's hair to all but stand on end. Like an echo to his gloomy prediction about the New York killer's fate, like a monster aroused and enraged by the statement, the earth gave a violent shake.

Renny was not a man easily scared. Yet he felt as if ice were in his blood. Not because the earth shook. Because of the other thing that happened—the uncanny thing.

The trembling of the cabin shook books off the shelves, and when they hit the floor there was absolutely no sound. Renny was so stunned by that phenomenon that he opened his mouth and swore. He did not hear himself.

Renny stamped his feet. He could not hear that. He yelled. He did not hear his own voice. He did feel the tickle as his vocal cords vibrated, and got a vibration against his eardrums, which he himself could understand.

It was incredible. All sound had ceased. It was impossible to make a noise.

Renny decided to try again, and opened his mouth and let out his best roar. In the middle of the bawl the weird spell suddenly ended, with the result that Renny all but deafened himself with his own howling. He fell silent and looked blank.

All of his captors laughed.

"That guy would make a good understudy to the 'Roar Devil," one of them said.

"Roar Devil!" Renny blinked. "Just what is this Roar Devil?"

The neat man smiled grimly. "Just what does the name suggest to you?"

"Don't be funny!" Renny rumbled.

"Power!" snapped the other. "That's what it suggests. And very fittingly, too, I will add. Power, such as no man has dreamed! And wealth. Infinite wealth! Other people's wealth, it is true. But as Bobby Burns did not say, 'wealth is wealth, for a' that.'"

"This don't make sense," Renny grumbled.

"Oh, yes it does, if you only knew," chuckled the other. "It makes very good sense. You have just felt the Roar Devil at work, taking the final steps that will crown him emperor of his realm. Or let us hope they crown him."

"I'll crown somebody before I'm through with this nutty business!" Renny promised. "Say, was that girl working for this Roar Devil?"

The neat man smirked. "Don't you ever draw conclusions from what you see?"

"Was she?" Renny demanded.

"You will put your hands behind you," directed the other. "We are going to tie them there."

Renny complied. It would have been insanity not to obey. They had their guns cocked.

"Did you," he was asked as he was being tied, "ever hear of Dove of Peace Zachies, or Dove Zachies, as he is called?"

Renny scowled. "Yeah."

"Has Doc Savage heard of him?"

"Yeah," Renny admitted. He was now bound tightly.

"Excellent," said the neat man. "Let us hope Doc Savage is still in his New York headquarters. The Roar Devil now has business with him."

Chapter VI

A NIGHT FOR TRADING

The small, plump, innocent-looking man with the gray beard stood in the doorway of Doc Savage's skyscraper headquarters. His hat was in his hand; he looked very meek.

"I am Dove Zachies," he said. "May I come in?"

Doc Savage showed no surprise as he moved the barrier of bulletproof plate glass aside and let Dove Zachies into the reception room.

"I have seen men who looked less like crooks," the bronze man said.

Zachies was cheerful and frank.

"I know better than to try to deceive you," he said. "I am a criminal in the eyes of the law, yes. But I have my own code of honor. I smuggle on a large scale, yes. I think tariffs are too high. I was in the liquor business during prohibition days. I did not believe in prohibition. I smuggle aliens. This is a free country, and why keep some out and let others in?"

"Did you come up here to argue about that?" Doc asked, without emotion.

Zachies shook his head solemnly.

"I came to ask your help," he announced.

"My help?"

"Not for myself," Zachies denied hastily. "I ask your help for the American public. Perhaps for the world."

"That sounds somewhat melodramatic," Doc Savage suggested.

40

Zachies became earnest, twisting his expensive hat in his hands.

"Have you heard of the Roar Devil?" he asked.

Doc Savage did not answer immediately, but moved over behind the massive inlaid table and seated himself. With seeming absent-mindedness, he rested a finger tip on the exquisite mosaic of the table top.

"The Roar Devil," he said, "has already made one attempt to kill me."

Zachies dropped his hat, and his rather characterless face registered vast astonishment.

"Then the Roar Devil has marked you for death!" he exclaimed. "He must have realized you were in his path!"

"His path to what?" Doc asked.

"Some mammoth crime," Dove Zachies replied. "I do not know what, and I hope you will believe me, even if that does sound strange."

Doc Savage tapped an inlay in the table top with the tip of a tendon-wrapped forefinger. His flake-gold eyes were steady on his visitor.

"Just what sent you to me?" he asked. "It was not a love of humanity, entirely."

Zachies managed to look injured, but he nodded.

"True," he said. "The Roar Devil asked me to merge my, ah—organization with his own. I refused. Now he is trying to kill me."

"You met the Roar Devil?" Doc asked sharply.

"I did not," Zachies denied. "He was only a voice over the telephone. A singing voice."

"Singing voice?"

"Exactly, Mr. Savage. And I can assure you that the singing of words will completely disguise a voice. It did this one, at any rate."

"Have you any concrete assistance to offer?" Doc asked.

"I certainly have. The Roar Devil is now haunting the mountains around Powertown, in upstate New York."

"How do you know that?"

Zachies leaned forward wearing an expression of intense seriousness.

"This Roar Devil is a monster who can do weird things, Mr. Savage. He bragged, when trying to enlist my aid, that he could destroy whole sections of the earth's surface. He said he would demonstrate on a small scale by shaking the earth around Powertown, so that the large dams there would be destroyed. He is doing that now, to impress me with his power. He is causing millions in damage and taking many lives, just to show me what he can do. Now I ask you, does that not make this Roar Devil a monster?"

Doc Savage asked, "Have you investigated the situation at Powertown?"

"I have," Zachies said promptly. "I was up there to-day—I mean, yesterday. I and my secretary—body-guard, I should say—were captured by a very unusual young woman named Retta Kenn, who I am positive is one of the Roar Devil's gang.

"Retta Kenn left us, probably while she went for more of the Roar Devil's men, or to tell her chief she had taken us. But some of my men, who had followed us, found us and released us. I was scared, let me tell you. I came directly to you."

Doc Savage said nothing for some moments. His forefinger absently stroked and tapped the inlay in the tabletop, as if keeping pace with his thoughts.

"Do you know anything more?" he queried.

"Only that I found a cabin with a young man in it who seemed completely paralyzed or hypnotized or something," said Zachies. "The cabin was owned by an inventor named D'Aughtell, and the young man was D'Aughtell's associate, Mort Collins. I got that information from searching the cabin. I think the Roar Devil has seized D'Aughtell and worked one of his spells on Mort Collins."

"What makes you think that?"

"The Roar Devil told me he could make a man into a living dead person. That describes Mort Collins's condition."

Doc Savage worried the tabletop with his finger.

"You say the Roar Devil has a singing manner of disguising his speech?"

"Exactly, Mr. Savage."

Doc gave the table several sharp taps.

"What about your cache, Zachies?" he demanded.

Zachies's mouth came widely open. He kept it open until he had put a long, pale cigar in it.

"I don't get you," he said.

"Is the Roar Devil not after your cache?" Doc asked.

"How could he be," Zachies said promptly. "I haven't got a cache. I don't even know what a cache is."

"A place where things are hidden," Doc supplied.

"I have nothing hidden," Zachies insisted.

Doc Savage studied him. The bronze man had been employing the information secured from the fellow who had tried to shoot him, while the latter was under the influence of the truth serum.

"I gather you are already after the Roar Devil," Zachies said at last.

"Right." Doc told him.

Zachies turned to the door. "Then I shall go." He paused to toss a card on the inlaid table. "There is my address. If you need the help of myself or any of my, ah—gang, just call on us."

"Thank you," Doc Savage said with just a trace of dryness, and escorted Zachies to the elevators.

It was with considerable haste, that the bronze man returned to the reception room. He went directly to the inlaid table and tapped on the particular bit of the inlay which he had been fingering previously.

A telegraph sounder clicked in response to the depressing of the inlay. But it did the clicking many stories below, in the basement of the skyscraper. The telegraph sounder was mounted in a resonator in Doc Savage's basement garage.

Two men were listening to the sounder, and from their expressions, it was evident both understood the code.

In appearance, these men differed about as much as two individuals could. One was a great, hairy fellow who came near bearing more resemblance to a bull ape than to a human being. He had practically no forehead, and a mouth which all but reached from ear to ear. He needed a shave, and his clothing looked like that of a tramp.

The other man was slender, lean-waisted, and his clothing was the ultimate in sartorial perfection. He carried a slender black cane.

"M-a-n i-s l-e-a-v-i-n-g n-o-w," translated the dapperly clad man, listening to the sounder. "F-o-l-l-o-w h-i-m."

"You don't hafta read that to me, Ham," complained the apish man, in a small voice that might have belonged to a child. "I learned to telegraph before Harvard ever heard of you."

"Shut up, you accident of nature!" the other said unkindly.

The two of them ran for a car. The gorilla of a fellow swerved to one side and grabbed up an animal which had been asleep on a small mound of cloth. It was a pig, an incredibly homely member of the poker family, with long legs, and ears that might have been meant for wings. It was by one enormous ear that the animal was being carried.

The dapper "Ham" glared. "You're not taking that insect along!"

"Watch me," said the owner of the terrible-looking hog. "And if you don't like it—swell!"

The two men traded throat-cutting looks. Then the nattily attired one grew pale and gripped his cane with both hands, separating it at the handle to disclose that it was in reality a sword cane with a vicious-looking blade. He seemed on the point of having a fit.

"Something you ate?" demanded the homely one.

"My coat!" Ham gurgled. "That nasty hog was sleeping on my new topcoat! Monk, you put him up to that!"

"The idea!" "Monk" sniffed. "I think more of this hog than to—— We better get going!"

They dived into a small coupe, Monk carrying the pig by one oversize ear. The coupe ran up an inclined drive and out onto the street.

Anxiously, the two men strained eyes at the few

pedestrians abroad at this hour of the morning. It was the homely Monk who first picked up Dove Zachies. Zachies was swinging jauntily along northward.

"There he is," Monk pointed out.

They followed Zachies.

"Throw that hog, you!" Ham commanded grimly, when they had covered two blocks.

"Nix," Monk refused. "Habeas Corpus is a blood-hog. You know all about bloodhounds, probably, but I'll bet this is the first bloodhog you ever seen——"

"Ugh!" Ham choked. "You'll buy me a new top-coat."

"I'll put that in my will," Monk said.

The quarreling continued, and at points it reached a heat which an unknowing observer would have been sure was to result in a fight. But fireworks never quite came off. As a matter of fact, the quarrel had been going on pretty continuously for years. The two were actually friends in their peculiar way.

Ham now mentioned the name of the archæologist and geologist of Doc Savage's group—William Harper Littlejohn.

"Where was Johnny to-night?" he demanded.

"Spouting his big words to a bunch of tomb robbers up at the Egyptian room of the museum," Monk said. "He should be due back at headquarters about now."

Ham attempted to kick the pig, Habeas Corpus.

"Cut that out!" Monk gritted.

"I'll cut his tail off right back of his ears, if he don't stop trying to chew on my shoes!" Ham snarled.

That quarrel lasted them until Dove Zachies, who had taken a taxicab, alighted from his hack far uptown. Zachies was evidently making sure that no single cab driver should take him all the way to where he was going, because he flagged a second taxi.

That one took him up into Westchester County, where there were many palatial estates. Zachies dismissed the hack, walked to the entrance of an estate, one encircled by a tall stone fence, and let himself through a massive iron gate.

Monk, Ham and the pig, Habeas, were close on his trail. Monk carried a leather hand bag which he had taken from the coupe.

"We gotta get in there," Monk decided. "Let's climb that wall."

"Let us listen at the gate first," Ham suggested.

They crept forward. When very near the gate, they heard voices. One was Dove Zachies, and the other probably the gatekeeper.

"Watch the gate closely," Dove Zachies was saying. "Things are getting very tough. Never mind the wall. No one can climb over that, because there is a fancy burglar alarm—wires strung on top of the wall, so that if any one gets near them, they make a bell ring. It's the latest thing, and it sure works."

"Nobody'll get by me," said a bull-like voice.

Monk and Ham withdrew a safe distance.

"Who wanted to climb the wall?" Ham asked sarcastically.

"Nuts to you," Monk told him. "How we gonna do this?"

Chapter VII

WATERLOO FOR TWO

The two men pondered in deep silence.

"We might," Ham suggested, "go up to the gate and pretend we had lost our way. The guard might come out to point the correct road. Then we could gang him."

"That guy didn't sound like a bird who would accommodate anybody that much," Monk retorted. "We gotta do better than that."

There were a few clouds in the sky now. It was very dark. Cars, moving swiftly on a distant highway, made long moaning noises. The aroma of spring was in the air. The pig, Habeas, grunted softly.

"I'll kick your gizzard out, hog," Ham gritted.

"Hah!" Monk breathed. "An idea!"

"Treat it gently," Ham advised. "It's in a strange place."

Monk ignored that, and seized Habeas. He pointed the pig's long snout at the gate.

"Bite 'em, pal!" he directed. "Go eat 'em up!"

Habeas trotted off. The night swallowed him completely. Then there was silence, more of it than Monk had expected. The cars on the distant highway seemed nearer, probably because the two men were straining their ears in the night.

Ham said, "I might have known that hog——"

There was a stifled gasp of pain from the gate. A man stamped, cursed, gasped again in pain.

Monk and Ham glided forward.

The guard was stamping around inside the estate, gritting profanity.

"Ouch!" he exploded. "What is this thing? Hell's bells! A hog!"

The next instant, the gate flew open. Habeas popped through, the irate guard close after him.

It was doubtful if the guard ever knew what happened to him. Monk's hard fist landed against his ear with the first swing. Ham caught him.

"Some hog," Monk said.

They listened for some minutes. There was no sign that the scuffle had been heard by any one in the large house which they could distinguish through the shrubbery and trees.

Monk carried the guard down the road, bound and gagged in businesslike fashion, left him, and returned. Ham was scratching one of Habeas Corpus's big ears, but desisted hastily when he discovered Monk.

"I knew you'd come to like that hog," Monk declared.

"I was just taming him," Ham said. "I'm going to cut his head off and have him served with fried eggs. I want him so I can catch him."

They crept through the shrubbery. The grass was close-cropped, the bushes tripped so that there was not much danger of running into stray branches. They found an open window. Both crawled through, after listening.

It was a sun room. Beyond it, they found a dark living room. Across that was an open, lighted door. They could see through it, and without getting too close could hear conversation coming through it.

The light came from a dining room. On the table stood bottles and glasses. Seven men were seated, some smoking.

Zachies, at the head of the table, said, "I tell you, boys, I fed this Doc Savage a sweet line of bull, and he lapped it up!"

One of the other men—none of them looked like a gentleman would care to meet in a dark alley—said,

"The bronze fellow has got the rep of being slicker than grease."

"Oh, I used a technique," Dove Zachies chuckled. "You see, I told just enough truth to make it sound right. And I gave him everything I knew about the Roar Devil."

"You said you left out the V. Venable Mear angle," reminded another of the men.

"Yeah." Dove Zachies leaned forward fiercely. "You know what I've decided?"

"What?"

"I've decided V. Venable Mear is the Roar Devil." Zachies leaned back and nodded vehemently. "That girl, Retta Kenn, is obviously working for the Roar Devil. And she had a telegram from this V. Venable Mear, directing her to grab me. Don't that kinda make it look like the Roar Devil is V. Venable Mear?"

"Just who is V. Venable Mear, Dove?" a man queried. "I don't make the name."

"Darned if I know who he is," said Dove Zachies. "But we're gonna find out. Bring me the telephone directory, somebody. Let's see if he's in there."

Some one interrupted, "But if V. Venable Mear is the Roar Devil, why not tell Doc Savage?"

Dove Zachies laughed.

"Because, if we can grab the Roar Devil, we can take over his game, see?" he pointed out. "It's big. The biggest thing in history, I'm telling you!"

"You ain't half smart," some one said, knowingly.

"Get me the telephone directory," ordered Zachies.

A man got up and walked into the room where Monk and Ham stood. He did it quickly, and there was no time for them to retreat. The only thing they could do was step hastily into darkened corners.

Monk, by the worst of luck, found he had taken up a position almost beside the telephone stand. The man from the other room marched up to the stand, bent over it and fumbled for the directory. Monk almost heaved a sigh of relief. The other was not going to see him!

Then the man hit Monk in the stomach. It was a

terrific blow! It would have sent most men to the hospital. It made Monk roar like a lion.

Monk hit the man who had struck him. The fellow was knocked out instantly, lifted and carried backward by the blow. He fell flat on his back in the door.

Bawling irately, Monk charged after him. The apish chemist scooped up a chair, and as he came through the lighted door, threw it at the chandelier. The lights went out in a jangling of glass, a popping of bulbs and a sizzling of blue electric flame.

Straight into the room Monk charged. He seized the table, ran it across the floor and pinned at least three men against a wall. He gave the table a final shove, which must have all but cut the victims in two.

There was a man underfoot. Monk jumped up and down on him. Some one fired a gun. Monk had gotten a bottle off the table. He threw it at the gun flash, and was rewarded by an end-of-the world groan.

Monk jumped up and down, bawled wrathfully, and charged wildly through the darkness in hopes of encountering another victim. A wall stopped him painfully.

"You missing link!" Ham shouted from the other room. "Get out of here while you can!"

Monk made one more foray in the darkness, found no one, and raced after Ham. They tumbled through the window together and set out across the grounds, the pig at their heels.

"Idiot!" Ham gritted. "That was a crazy thing to do!"

"That guy hit me in the place where I put all my food," Monk growled. "I value that spot."

"We've got information for Doc," Ham gasped. "That stuff about V. Venable Mear——"

"Blazes!" Monk howled. "What's this!"

"This" was the figure of a woman. She had flashed up ahead of them and was racing madly for the gate.

The fleeing girl cast a wild glance over her shoulder. It was doubtful if she could see much in the darkness. Only the fact that there was an electric light at the gate permitted Monk and Ham to discern her.

She reached the gate, whipped through, then slammed the heavy portals.

"Hey!" Monk bawled. "Don't do that! We're clearing out of here, too!"

The girl heard. She stopped, wheeled, and began fighting the gate. She was trying to get it open for them. But the lock was of a spring variety which foiled her.

Behind them, a submachine gun emitted a ripping volley. Monk and Ham hurled themselves flat and began to crawl. They could hear slugs snarling through the surrounding shrubbery.

Then the bullets began digging at the stone wall and clanging on the gate. The girl did the only safe thing. She wheeled and fled.

Brilliant floodlights came on. These were located along the wall and placed so cleverly that every square yard of the estate was lighted.

Dove Zachies and the remnants of his gang charged forward.

"Jig's up!" Monk groaned.

Monk and Ham were both lying in plain view, now that the lights were on. They both had machine pistols. Using them would have been inviting suicide.

Dove Zachies came up, glaring. He had evidently familiarized himself with Doc Savage's organization, probably from such newspaper pictures as had been printed.

"Monk and Ham, they call you," he snarled. Then he waved an arm. "Get that woman!"

Men raced off.

Ten minutes later, they were all back.

"She got away," one imparted. "Had a car waiting down the road."

"*Ahr-r-r!*" muttered Dove Zachies.

"Who was she, Dove?" a man queried.

"Retta Kenn," said Dove Zachies.

Monk and Ham were taken into the house. The guard they had overpowered, bound and gagged was found and released. Every one sat around listening anxiously for some evidence that the shooting had moved a neighbor to call the police. Nothing happened.

"I bought this place because it was isolated," Dove Zachies sighed. Then he came over to Monk and Ham, both of whom were now secured with bright new handcuffs.

"So Doc Savage didn't swallow my line as well as I thought?" Zachies growled. "Just how much does Savage know?"

"I can't hear you," Monk squeaked. "I'm kinda deaf at times."

That threw Dove Zachies into a spasm of rage, the violence of which puzzled Monk, who had no way of knowing as yet that Zachies had been taken in the previous day when Retta Kenn put over a very good pretense of being deaf.

Zachies put out his rather weak-looking jaw.

"Know what I'm gonna do with you two bright boys?" he gritted.

"I ain't a mind reader, either," Monk advised.

"I'm gonna use you to persuade Doc Savage to really go to town on this Roar Devil," Zachies advised.

Monk squinted small eyes at him. "Yeah? How?"

"I'm gonna call up Doc Savage and yell over the telephone that the Roar Devil is attackin' my estate here."

"Then what?" Monk asked curiously.

"Then I'm gonna shoot you two," Zachies advised. "I'll tell Doc Savage that the Roar Devil did it. What do you think of that? It'll make Doc Savage real anxious to get the Roar Devil, won't it? It'll stir him up, won't it?"

"It'll stir him up," Monk admitted.

Dove Zachies walked over and picked up the telephone.

Chapter VIII

THE DEAD MAN'S VOICE

The telephones in Doc Savage's office were connected to buzzers which had various tones. The one which sounded now was unusually shrill, something resembling the prolonged squeak of a mouse.

An extremely tall and amazingly thin man in Doc Savage's reception room moved toward the instrument. This man's appearance was rather startlingly like that of a skeleton with a very thin coating of skin and flesh. He was Johnny.

"The communication may not be of memorabilian consequence," he said solemnly.

"I will take it," Doc Savage said.

The bronze man swung over and scooped up the telephone, which was one of a bank of several, all numbered.

"I wish to speak with Doc Savage, please," said a voice over the wire.

Doc Savage did not change expression, but into the room, for the briefest of moments, came the low, exotic trilling sound which was his own peculiar characteristic, the sound which he made in moments of mental excitement.

The words over the telephone had come in a peculiar singing manner of delivery. And Dove Zachies had said this was the method used by the Roar Devil to disguise his speech.

"This is Doc Savage," the bronze man admitted.

There followed a pause of such duration that it seemed the voice of the Roar Devil was not going to

53

sound again. Then singsong words came out of the receiver.

"Please do not interrupt what I have to say, and listen carefully," directed the voice. "This is the Roar Devil. I have your man, Renny. He is unharmed, except for minor bruises. Nor will he be harmed if you follow certain instructions."

Doc Savage took the receiver away from his ear enough for the bony Johnny to hear the words. Johnny nodded, backed away and picked up another instrument, where he promptly began trying to trace the call.

"Dove Zachies is the man I really want," continued the Roar Devil.

There was a slight pause after that, as if for emphasis.

"Get Zachies, and I will trade your man Renny for him," the Roar Devil went on. "I will know when you have received Zachies. I have sources of information. I will then get in touch with you and arrange for the trade. Now, you will want proof that I have Renny."

There was a short silence. Then Renny's booming voice, angry and unmistakable, came out of the receiver.

"I know about this trade he's trying to make, Doc," said Renny's roar. "Tell him to go to blazes! But watch your step! And don't kid yourself that this Roar Devil isn't dangerous!"

The wire rattled as the connection was broken.

Doc Savage, still holding the receiver, spun on gaunt Johnny.

"Get it?"

Johnny said over the other telephone, "Thank you immensely," and hung up.

"Supermalagorgeous," he told Doc Savage. "Thanks to the previous arrangements we made with the telephone company, we got results."

"The call came from where?"

"From a place in Westchester County."

Doc Savage's trilling, like the note of some exotic

tropical bird, came out briefly. It persisted, a delicate vibration almost too nebulous for the ear to catch, then faded into infinity.

The bony Johnny looked puzzled. Doc explained.

"That address," said the bronze man, "is Dove Zachies's country estate."

"Dove Zachies—I'll be superamalgamated! Indeed I will!"

Doc Savage said, "Come on!"

A policeman stopped them once as they drove north. He was a rookie, and the special license plates on Doc Savage's lean, gloomy-colored roadster meant nothing to him, he said. Making eighty miles an hour on a boulevard did. The license plates meant something, too, after he called his district chief. He was all apologies as he let them go.

Doc Savage and Johnny left the somber roadster some distance from their destination, walked a hundred yards and found the coupe in which Monk and Ham had ridden.

Johnny looked the car over and said, "An unpropitious omen."

Doc Savage did not comment.

"There is a possibility that Dove Zachies is the Roar Devil, and trying to cover it up," Doc Savage said.

"He came to me and said he wanted me to get the Roar Devil," Doc said. "He would hardly sic us on himself."

"There are ways of condoning that angle," Johnny said. "He might have phenagled to steer suspicion from himself."

"It may come out in the wash," Doc told him.

The gate to Dove Zachies's pretentious estate was open.

There was a dead man inside the gate.

The dead man sat with his back to a tree. He had both hands clamped over his middle, and the hands were red with a redness that had leaked through them and had soaked the man's legs and puddled between them.

A gun and a flashlight lay near the man. The gun was a Luger, and the man had a Luger holster under his coat. There was also a worn place at his belt where the flashlight had dangled from a snap and ring. There was a package of French cigarettes in the dead man's pockets, and French cigarette butts about the gate. Some of the stubs had been there for days.

"Watchman," Doc Savage said. "Do not try to move him. They used a knife on him and he's about ready to fall apart."

Bright lights inside the house made it look big and white. The front door was off its hinges. Two of the front windows were broken out.

There was another dead man inside the door, and he had been shot. The stitched pattern on his soggy chest indicated a machine gun.

In the dining room, they found two coats hanging neatly on the back of a chair. Johnny looked at them. He used very small words when he spoke.

"Ham's coat," he said, and pointed at the other garment. "This one is Monk's. Look at the manner in which Monk's is torn. They had trouble. Probably they were captured."

Doc Savage went on through the house, opened a door, and was unexpectedly confronting the cloudy night, although the door had opened into what had once been a kitchen. The whole rear of the house was gone, blown away.

The bronze man surveyed the damage appraisingly, noting that the floor had been blown downward in a manner which indicated the explosion had occurred inside the room.

"Grenade," he said. "A large one."

"I'll be superamalgamated!" Johnny made vague gestures, and fingered the monocle which dangled from a ribbon and had been stowed in the handkerchief pocket of his coat. "This explosion! It must have been heard fifteen miles away!"•

He glanced about, then indicated numerous empty cartridges.

"Shooting and no one heard it and gave an

alarm," he said. "Ditto for the explosion. That is strange."

Johnny did not ordinarily speak this many sentences without at least one which could not be translated without a dictionary. Possibly that was because his big words were a form of showmanship, and he knew better than to try to impress Doc Savage.

Doc Savage replied nothing, but went back into the dining room. He turned off the lights.

From a pocket, the bronze man drew a device which might have been a miniature camera, except that the large lense was almost black in hue. He flicked a switch on the side of this. A faint singing sound came from the apparatus, a note which might have been made by a high-pitched vibrator.

Doc pointed the instrument about the room. It gave off no visible light. But several times, objects glowed weirdly under its spell. Two stray aspirin tablets, for instance, became small phosphorescent spots.

Then a sentence in writing leaped out distinctly.

Doc Savage went closer to the writing with the apparatus—it was merely a lantern for the projecting of so-called "black light," or ultra-violet rays, of a wave length invisible to a normal human eye.

The writing was in secret chalk, a chalk which took advantage of the property, well known to scientists, which many substances have of phosphorescing, or glowing, when exposed to the black light. The appearance of this chalk was innocent, and it left a mark almost impossible to detect by ordinary methods. Doc Savage's aides each carried it.

The letters were big and distinctive.

"Monk's handwriting," Doc said.

The bronze man and Johnny studied the words:

ZACHIES THINKS V. VENABLE MEAR IS ROAR DEVIL.
ALL STILL A MYSTERY.
WE GOT GLOMMED.

"He has a quaint way of saying he and Ham were taken prisoner," Johnny said dryly. "Wonder what happened after he wrote that."

Doc Savage began going over the house with more care. Bullets had made holes in the windows or taken the glass out entirely. A man had bled a little lake in one room. Three times the bronze man found bullets which were flattened and mutilated as if they had encountered bulletproof vests.

The ultra-violet lantern was still in use. On the basement floor, it unearthed another message:

> FIREWORKS—ROAR DEVIL, I THINK.
> ZACHIES GOING KILL US AND BLOW.

There was no more at that spot. Johnny was a tower of gloom as thy continued their hunt. Adjoining the cellar was a semibasement garage. In front of the door, as if he had been dropped there while the door was opened—the door had been smashed—was written:

> FRYING PAN INTO FIRE—ROAR DEVIL GOT US.

Johnny gasped delightedly, "So Zachies did not kill them, after all. Probably he did not have time."

Doc Savage moved into the garage.

"This seems to be a continued story," he said, and pointed.

Glowing letters came out under the ultra-violet lamp:

> ROAR DEVIL OVERHEARD SAYING HE USED
> TELEPHONE RECORD WITH——

That must have been interrupted, for it was unfinished.

"What could he have been trying to say?" Johnny pondered aloud.

"Probably he was trying to tell me he had overheard enough to know that the Roar Devil employed a telephone record with Renny's voice on it when he called me to offer Renny in exchange for Dove Zachies," Doc Savage said.

Johnny started as if he had been kicked.

"I'll be super—you knew that?" he exploded.

"You have heard phonographic transcriptions played over the radio," Doc told him. "There is a certain unmistakable scratching made by the needle. Probably the Roar Devil did not think it would be strong enough to detect over the telephone."

On the other side of the garage was the last word from Monk:

> ZACHIES ESCAPED.
> ROAR DEVIL TAKING US.
> INVESTIGATE V. VENABLE MEAR.

Johnny commented on the situation when they were running toward their car to go back to New York City.

"It does not seem that Dove Zachies is the Roar Devil, after all, does it?"

Doc Savage did not voice any answer.

The telephone directory had it:

> MEAR V. VENABLE, cml pscyt, 1 Merving Alley, NOrth 8-4001.

Johnny absently passed his monocle over the printed line. The monocle was unwearable, being a magnifying glass of no small power. Johnny used a glass often in his profession of archæologist, and carried it as a monocle for convenience.

"That abbreviation 'cml pscyt' must mean——"

"Criminal psychologist," Doc Savage completed for him. "That sounds interesting."

"Number One Merving Alley," Johnny said. "Five minutes should see us in that section of the metropolis."

An outsider might have mistaken Merving Alley for just what its name implied, a dump. It looked the part, except possibly that the buildings were too clean, being whitewashed, and the pavement was very sanitary. No native New Yorker would have made the error, however.

Merving Alley was "class." Three of the world's leading artists lived there, some painters of equal importance, and a famous international banker. Those old buildings had once been stables, but the interiors had long since been remodeled at the expenditure of several million dollars. The residents were persons who found themselves bored by the ordinary, and who had money enough to go in for the extraordinary.

Number One was a whitewashed box of bricks which was absolutely windowless. As far as could be seen there was only one small door, and that of heavy timbers. It was a barn door.

"How do we conduct our camisado?" Johnny queried. "Rush the place?"

"The gentleman might not know we are interested in him," the bronze man reminded. "Why add the information to his worries. The Chinese have a proverb: 'When there is rain without clouds meeting the eye, the wisest man may get wet.'"

"I see," said Johnny. "We rain on him, but we don't cloud up."

It was not yet dawn. The corner street lamp was furnishing them enough light to study the square house.

"An alley at the back," Doc reminded.

In the alley, the bronze man drew a silk cord, a grappling hook attached to the end, and tossed it upward after a moment of careful calculation. The grappling hook was collapsible, and covered with soft rubber, so that the noise it made scarcely reached their ears. It must have hung over the edge of the roof. Doc pulled, testing. It hung.

He went up.

Johnny mounted next. He found the bronze man looking down through an enormous turret of a skylight. Johnny hurried over. He looked down.

At first it seemed that he was peering into a pool of soft flame; then his eyes accustomed themselves and he could make out a room, done in red from top to bottom. There was nothing but red in the room. Even the paper which lay on the great desk in the middle of the fantastic study was red.

Johnny drew back. A peculiar expression was on his long, bony face. He blinked his eyes slowly.

"Strange place," he mumbled. "Sort of a phantasmagoria in erubescence——" He trailed his voice off and scratched his head. He smiled slightly. He was not a man who smiled often. Suddenly, he threw back his head.

He emitted a deafening peal of laughter and fell flat on his face.

The next instant, Doc Savage did almost exactly the same thing.

Neither man moved after he had fallen.

Chapter IX

THE DEVILS COLLIDE

The man looked ageless. Rather, he looked as if he had gotten old to a point where he no longer showed the years. His skin was like sandpaper from which hard rubbing had erased the sand. His eyes had no particular color. They might have been little cellophane bags with unclear water in them.

He opened his mouth when he breathed, and the teeth that showed were so strong and white-looking that they were obviously artificial. Yet he was not stooped very much. Nor was his step feeble.

He had a head of amazing bigness above the ears. It was white and hairless and somehow made one think of a tremendous skull. When he came into the red room, the red light somehow gave him the look of a devil.

He said, "You two have been unconscious about half an hour, if that interests you."

His voice was a thing of unusual beauty. It was an operatic voice.

"Thank you immeasurably," said the bony Johnny.

Doc Savage said nothing.

They were seated on chairs, stout steel chairs, and they were held by handcuffs to the chairs. Doc Savage could break ordinary handcuffs. He had not broken these. He had tried.

Doc and Johnny had recovered their senses some ten minutes before.

"It is hardly necessary to explain that I did this because I found you prowling on the roof of my house," the ageless man announced. "My burglar alarms, and very excellent they are, too, showed you there."

He waited, apparently for the two men to say something, but they were silent, and he rubbed his hands together and smiled. The skin on his hands looked so dry that it was strange that it did not crackle, seemingly.

"There are tiny gas vents in the roof," he said. "The gas is both colorless and odorless. But I believe that you, Doc Savage, are versed enough in chemistry to have already guessed the nature of the gas. You see, I recognized you the instant I came near you. Unfortunately, however, that was not until after you were senseless." He bowed to Johnny. "You are William Harper Littlejohn. I am indeed glad to meet such a learned man."

Johnny gave him only a steady stare.

The ageless man bowed.

"I am V. Venable Mear," he said. "I presume you came to see me. The roof of my house is of no use in gaining the roofs of other houses, for it sets apart. So I presume you were on my roof to see me."

He looked at them expectantly as he paused, and when they did not answer, smiled, shook his head and continued.

"Indeed, I am glad to meet you," he said. "I am a man of the sciences myself, although I have never put my knowledge to spectacular uses. I am a criminologist. I study crime and criminals. Study them, you understand, to devise methods of combating them."

"You," Johnny rapped suddenly, "are the Roar Devil!"

V. Venable Mear smiled, rubbed his hands and seemed about to bow, when the door snapped open.

Retta Kenn came in.

"There's the devil to pay!" she snapped. "Dove Zachies is outside with a gang. He thinks you are the Roar Devil. He's going to get you!"

The girl was excited, but certainly not scared. She gave the impression of being rather delighted about the whole thing.

There was a gun in V. Venable Mear's hand. Just how it had gotten there was a mystery. He was very fast.

"Tell me about it," he suggested, as if there was all the time in the world.

"I went to Dove Zachies's place in Westchester to pick up his trail, as you directed," said Retta Kenn. "I saw Dove Zachies seize Doc Savage's two men, Monk and Ham. I saw the Roar Devil's men attack Zachies and drive him away and capture Monk and Ham."

"Did you see the Roar Devil?" V. Venable Mear demanded.

"No." She shook her head. "He was not with his men. I overheard enough to know that. Then Zachies escaped, and I trailed him and learned he was coming here. I tried to beat him. His men were getting out of cars at the corner as I entered the house."

"You should have called me for orders," snapped Mear.

"Why?" countered the girl.

"Because I would have had you follow the Roar Devil's men," Mear informed her.

"You told me you wanted Dove Zachies."

"My client wants Zachies," corrected V. Venable Mear. "I have taken a personal interest in this affair. For that reason, I want the Roar Devil."

"I'm no mind reader," said the girl.

V. Venable Mear rubbed his hands together. No sound had as yet come from the street door.

Mear turned on Doc Savage suddenly.

"Can you talk?" he asked.

"On occasion," Doc Savage admitted, without emotion.

"Who is the Roar Devil?" Mear demanded.

Doc Savage made no answer.

"What is he after?" Mear persisted.

Doc returned him silence.

Mear sighed. "I fear I do not have a trustworthy face. It must be my age. It is hard for an old man to look honest."

The girl said dryly, "And while we stand here singing songs, our enemies gather without. Brother, you'd better look in your hat for rabbits."

V. Venable Mear gave no indication of having heard her. He looked at Doc.

"You think I'm a crook, don't you?" he demanded. "An old shyster with a lot of words—isn't that what you think?"

"You know what the Roar Devil is after, don't you?" Doc Savage asked.

"I do," said V. Venable Mear.

"You know why he and Dove Zachies are fighting," Doc asked.

"I do," admitted Mear.

"And you know *who* the Roar Devil is," Doc announced.

"I do," said Mear. "At least, I have an idea that will hold water."

"I think *you* are the Roar Devil," Johnny put in suddenly.

V. Venable Mear laughed. He came over and unlocked Doc Savage and Johnny.

While Doc and Johnny were moving arms and legs to restore circulation, V. Venable Mear moved over to the girl, stood with his back turned so that his lips could not be read, and said something into her ear in a voice so low they did not catch even the swishing of the whisper.

The girl walked rapidly toward the rear of the house and was lost to sight.

"Come," V. Venable Mear said.

He led Doc and Johnny to the front door and opened it.

The street was full of motionless bodies.

"I'll be superamalgamated!" Johnny exploded.

"Exactly," said V. Venable Mear. "You see, I kept you in there talking until the gas blew out of the street. It was the same kind of gas which overcame you, and there is not much wind, so it took a little time. Incidentally, I have always wondered how the trick would work. Quite effective, don't you think?"

Johnny bent a studious stare on V. Venable Mear. "You are a metempirical personality," he said.

V. Venable Mear smiled, rubbed his hands. "On the contrary, I am a man who makes his living by studying criminals and ways of combating them. This gas and the method of its distribution is my invention. I shall sell it to banks. Yes, I shall put on quite an advertising campaign. It is against my nature to seek publicity, but I think I shall now call in the newspaper reporters. This should get me more advertising than I could buy with a million dollars."

Johnny looked at Doc. "I can't make this fellow out."

V. Venable Mear smiled more widely and executed a sharp bow.

"May I introduce myself again as the man——"

V. Venable Mear screamed and fell down.

Simultaneously, or almost so, there was a sound as if some one had whistled, and close on the heels of that, a lip-popping noise. Tumbling after that, so close that the noises blended, came the whooping echoes of a shot.

Johnny started, "I'll be super——"

Doc Savage knocked him down. Down and back, through the door into the house. And the bronze man followed him, bending over and getting the still-falling Johnny by the shoulders and dragging him on into the house.

During that split-second interval, a thunder of shots rolled in the street and bullets made unearthly and hideous noises as they mutilated the door and the door jamb.

V. Venable Mear was screaming—and rolling. There seemed to be blind insanity to his rolling, for it had carried him out in the street.

Johnny made something like a move to go after him.

"You couldn't make it," Doc told him. "Nobody could, unless they were in a tank. And even then, I wouldn't be so sure."

They could see two of the flashing guns. They

were on top of a dwelling across the street. There were at least a dozen other guns going.

Doc Savage and Johnny moved backward. There was a passage inside the door, and it sheltered them.

They stood there until two men ran into view. They wore clumsy bullet-proof capes, steel helmets, and kept their heads down to protect their faces as much as possible. They worked like soldiers making a charge.

The two seized V. Venable Mear.

"Be sure he don't get hurt!" one of the men gasped.

They dragged Mear away.

Doc and Johnny retreated. There was nothing more for them to do here. They could hear shouting, some one ordering a charge on the house.

Johnny had a machine pistol. He clipped a drum of tear-gas bullets into it and emptied them into the street. That held off the assault for a while.

They found the rear door. It was open, inviting. The surroundings were very dark. Doc Savage stopped Johnny before he could go out.

"Wait," Doc advised.

He went back.

"Young lady!" he called.

There was no answer from Retta Kenn, no sound to indicate that she was in the house.

There was a kitchen, and from a shelf the bronze man got several ripe tomatoes. Back at the rear door, he tore off bits of the tomatoes and tossed them carefully, one piece at a time. They were soft, and because they did not roll after they fell, they sounded much like footsteps.

A revolver set up a loud *bang-bang-bang!* Bullets chopped and snarled where the tomato fragments had followed.

Johnny let a bullfiddle moan out of his machine pistol. A man cried out. His body fell heavily. There was no other sound from the alley, but much yelling around in front.

Doc Savage and Johnny were not interfered with as they ran away.

They loitered in the vicinity. The raiders gathered up Dove Zachies's men, who were unconscious in the street. They did not get Dove Zachies. They wanted him. There was much shouted urging to find his body, but they went without it.

They took V. Venable Mear.

Cars were waiting, big fast machines which boomed into the street and picked up every one. A radio police patrol car barged into the thick of it, to have the wheels all but shot out from under it. The startled policemen fell down a basement areaway, dragging one of their number who had taken bullets through his legs.

The raiders betook themselves away.

Not once did Doc Savage detect a trace of the girl. He and Johnny left the vicinity quietly.

Chapter X

TRAIL

The sunrise was resplendent, its coloring an artist's dream. But not many city dwellers get up to see sunrises.

Johnny sat in Doc Savage's skyscraper office and frowned at an inspiring display of pale rosy light upon nebulous clouds, skyscraper spires, harbor water, ships. Doc Savage was going over the newspapers. They had broken out their largest type:

MAMMOTH MYSTERY RAID
STAGED BY GUNMAN HORDE

The story below kept pretty close to the facts as they had come to the attention of the reporters. There was no mention of Dove Zachies, Roar Devil or Retta Kenn.

PURPOSE UNKNOWN

There was some conjecture below that which had come from some alert rewrite man's brain.

GET-AWAY CARS ALL STOLEN

Seven cars had been found. The policemen who had come upon the scene had done a good job of getting license numbers. To Doc Savage's knowledge, there had been only seven cars.

V. Venable Mear known
TO POLICE

They knew him well and favorably, it seemed. He had once served as instructor in the New York police school, had even been a policeman, and was now a big-time consulting criminologist, one of the practical kind, not a student of theory. Mear was being sought, because his safety was feared for.

POSSIBLE MOTIVE

Maybe crooked enemies made by Mear in the course of his crime-combating activities, had made off with him. But why had they sent a young army for the purpose?

Doc Savage put the newspapers down.

"Have you a prognostication concerning identity of the raiders?" big-worded Johnny suggested.

"The Roar Devil's men," Doc said.

"I think so, too." Johnny frowned. "But what about the girl?"

"She fled," Doc said. "Or Mear sent her away. You recall that he spoke to her, and she left just after he turned us loose."

"She was working for Mear," Johnny murmured, forgetting his big words in his gloom. "I wonder if she was working for the Roar Devil, too?"

"Time may tell," Doc replied.

Johnny grimaced.

"I hope time tells what is behind this. There must be something big at stake. Those fellows were desperate, not afraid of killing. Criminals don't stage things like that in this day, unless they have plenty of reason. And where are Monk and Ham?"

"And Renny," Doc said. "I telephoned Powertown. Renny walked out of the Powertown Municipal Office Building after pointing out that some one had been eavesdropping on the meetings. He has not been seen since."

"What about the eavesdropper?"

"A young woman named Retta Kenn, who answers the description of the girl who was with V. Venable Mear," Doc said. "That information came from the hotel in Powertown where she was doing her listening-in."

"I doubt if we ever see her again," Johnny grumbled. "Maybe she was killed in all of that shooting at Mear's place."

Knuckles tapped the door. Doc opened the panel.

Retta Kenn came in, and bumped her nose against the sheet of transparent bulletproof glass.

"I'll be superamalgamated!" gasped Johnny.

Retta Kenn ran her hands over the glass panel and did not find a way past it.

"I thought V. Venable had all of the silly gadgets in the world," she said. "How do you pass this thing— or don't you?"

Doc Savage looked at her closely. He had studied psychology most of his life. He knew all of the character traits of men and could spot the small things which tell whether a man is honest or not, whether he is friend or foe. He could tell an average criminal at a glance, and usually spotted the cleverest of men in a short time.

He could not with certainty tell the first thing about a woman, and he knew it.

He lifted Johnny's machine pistol from its holster, held it in the general direction of the girl, and brought her in. He walked her directly to the laboratory and stood her in front of a large screen. He turned a switch.

A big mechanical box behind the girl began to buzz. Doc walked around on the other side of the screen.

It was a big X-ray machine, and the skeleton of the girl stood out beautifully on the fluoroscope screen. A gun showed just above her left knee.

The gun was probably shoved into the top of a stocking.

"It is common practice to examine bombs in that way," Doc said dryly.

"Well, I like that!" she snapped, suddenly understanding what he had done.

"Is the gun necessary?" he asked.

She hesitated. "Maybe not here."

She handed it over.

"Now," Doc said. "What is it?"

Her voice sounded as if she were thrilled—not in a cheerful way, as if she were enjoying herself, but as if she were getting an enormous kick out of things, and would do the same thing over again if she had the chance.

She seemed about to answer, but it chanced that Johnny walked in front of the X-ray and the girl was in a position where she could view the fluoroscopic screen.

"You don't look much different," she told the incredibly gaunt Johnny.

"Why are you here?" Doc Savage repeated.

"Help for V. Venable," she said. "He needs it. I want you to find him. I think the Roar Devil has him. And I want you to catch Dove Zachies for me."

"All right," Doc Savage told her. "But we'll start with something else."

"With what?"

"With what is behind all this."

"I'll tell you," Retta Kenn said.

"Who is the Roar Devil?" Johnny demanded.

"Somebody who can shake the earth," the girl said. "Somebody who can stop all sound. Somebody who has a vast organization of desperate criminals at his command."

"His name," Doc suggested.

"My friend, I'd like very well to know that myself," Retta Kenn replied.

"Imperspicuousity," said Johnny.

"I went to school," the girl snapped. "But they didn't have that word."

"Clear as mud," Johnny translated. "I am referring, of course, to the fact that you do not know——"

"All right, all right," she said rapidly. "I know you two probably think I'm working for the Roar Devil.

But here's the low-down. I am Retta Kenn, a young woman who has more money than sense. I get a kick out of excitement. So I work for V. Venable Mear, who has lots of exciting times chasing criminals and things like that."

She paused, eyed them hopefully, then shrugged.

"Two poker faces if I ever saw any. Well, a week ago, V. Venable Mear gets a call from a mysterious person who said that his name was April Fifth——"

"What?" Doc interrupted.

"April Fifth," snapped the girl. "I know it sounds goofy, but he said his name was April Fifth, and he wanted us to find Dove Zachies, seize him and deliver him like so much merchandise. It was queer. But April Fifth offered ten thousand dollars for the job, and V. Venable needed money, so we took the job."

She sighed loudly.

"We certainly took something! We trail Dove Zachies, trying to seize him. But you would be surprised how alert those bodyguards of his are. Then we begin to learn things by eavesdropping. I'm some eavesdropper."

She squinted at them.

"We learn Dove Zachies is in deadly fear of this Roar Devil. That is why the bodyguards were on the job so strong. The Roar Devil and Zachies are fighting. The Roar Devil wants something that Zachies has. That something must be in the mountains around Powertown. That must be where the earth shaking and those dams breaking and those queer periods of absolute silence and those roaring noises come in. I haven't been making heads nor tails of it all, and that's the truth. Yesterday, I got Zachies, but some one must have turned him loose. Does that explain me satisfactorily?"

"There is the matter of eavesdropping on the Powertown city fathers," Doc said.

"Oh, that." She nodded as if she had forgotten. "V. Venable told me to do that. He said he was interested in this Roar Devil, and he thought it was some one in Powertown. He thinks it is the Powertown mayor, Leland Ricketts."

"Leland Ricketts," Doc said slowly. "Why Ricketts?"

"I don't know," said the girl. "But V. Venable suspects him."

"This all you know?"

"Absolutely."

"Dove Zachies told us the Roar Devil was a mastermind with some fiendish scheme, and that he was destroying those dams near Powertown in an effort to convince him, Zachies, that he had better throw in with the Roar Devil," Johnny said.

"Did you believe him?" the girl countered.

"No," Johnny admitted.

Retta Kenn said, "I think we had better give Powertown a whirl. What do you men think?"

"I think you might explain how you managed to escape V. Venable Mear's house during that raid," Doc told her.

"Oh, that. Simple. V. Venable sent me for the police. Ask the police. I called that radio car which was first on the scene."

"We go to Powertown," Doc told her.

The Powertown Municipal Airport was on the south side of the city, well down on the floor of the valley, and coming from it into town carried one past the new Powertown schoolhouse and the new Powertown Municipal Hospital.

A small boy, probably tardy, was tearing for the door of the schoolhouse when Doc, Johnny and Retta Kenn rode past in a taxicab.

In front of the hospital a police car, siren screaming, frightened the taxi driver into the curb. The police car whined into the hospital grounds. The taxi driver craned his neck.

"Dog-gone!" he said. "Something's happened!"

"Wait," Doc Savage directed, and got out of the machine and walked into the hospital grounds.

There was a crowd around two dead men on the hospital lawn.

"They brought them out here and killed them,"

some one said. "It was a dirty thing, killing two helpless men like that!"

Doc Savage's unusual height permitted him to
look over the crowd and he saw that the two dead
men were encased in white hospital nightgowns.

"Who are they?" he asked a man at his elbow.

"The two engineers hired to see what was making
the dams break," the bystander replied. "The two
guys were found in the mountains, hypnotized or
paralyzed or something. They were brought to the
hospital."

The man stopped as if he considered he had
finished the story.

"They seem to be dead," Doc reminded him.

The other demanded, "Mean to say you haven't
heard what happened?"

"No."

"A car drove up," the man explained. "It was
jammed with men and guns. They walked into the
hospital, leaving one of their men in the car. They
dragged the two engineers out and killed them. But
that ain't the funniest thing."

"What is funnier?" Doc asked politely.

"Nobody could hear anything when it was going
on," said the spectator. "The guns weren't silenced,
but when they went off and killed the two engineers,
nobody heard it. It was the funniest thing."

"Any of the killers recognized?"

"They had masks."

Doc Savage went back to the taxicab, and
Johnny and Retta Kenn, who had joined him, also
returned. They got in and the hack carried them on.

"The Roar Devil," Retta Kenn said decisively.

"No doubt," Doc agreed.

"Getting scared," the girl continued. "Those two
engineers must have come onto something in the
mountains, something that would help us corner the
Roar Devil. He was afraid you would bring them out
of whatever ailed them, and they would talk. What
do you suppose was wrong with them?"

Doc Savage said nothing. Apparently, he had not
heard.

"What do you think was wrong with them?" the girl repeated.

The bronze man's seeming deafness persisted.

"Say, you!" the girl said belligerently. "If you think because you're a big-shot and the little tin idol of a lot of people, you can——"

Johnny punched her in the side. His finger was bony and the punch anything but gentle.

The girl choked, "Say, you——"

"You shut up!" Johnny suggested. "You're making a fool out of yourself."

"I am, am I?" She twisted around as if to take a swing at him.

At that instant, the taxi stopped in front of the Powertown Municipal Office Building.

Two policemen ran out. They seized the girl, hauled her out of the cab and put handcuffs on her wrists.

Chapter XI

HIS HONOR

Retta Kenn did not seem to care with whom she fought. She was very mad, and she still seemed to be enjoying herself. She kicked one policeman's shins. When he yelped and bent over, she hit him in the eye. The other policeman wrestled her down and sat on her.

His Honor, Mayor Leland Ricketts, fluttered down the high steps that led into the Municipal Office Building. Mayor Ricketts looked resplendent in winged collar, cutaway and striped trousers. His gardenia was enormous. He struck an attitude.

"Excellent!" he exclaimed stentoriously. "It does my heart good to observe such sterling attention to duties on the part of the hired servants of the law. I commend you——"

He saw Doc Savage. His mouth hung open.

Johnny was watching Mayor Leland Ricketts when he saw Doc Savage, and he tried to read the mayor's emotions. He was not very successful. It is hard to read the faces of most fat men, except for the eyes. In Mayor Leland Ricketts's eyes, Johnny thought he saw some emotion that was not pleasant. Certainly it seemed more than mere surprise at seeing the giant bronze man.

"Doc Savage!" Ricketts said sharply. "It is time you were getting here."

The bronze man seemed not to note the tartness in his honor's voice. He indicated Johnny and said, "This is my associate, William Harper Littlejohn."

The girl, still being held down by the policeman, said from the sidewalk, "What about me?"

His honor answered that.

"You," he told her, "are going to jail."

"On what charge?" Retta Kenn snapped.

"Eavesdropping," said Mayor Ricketts.

"Hah!" the girl exploded. "Since when did that become a crime? I know the law. You can book me on a nuisance charge, and I'll be out on bond in five minutes!"

Mayor Ricketts frowned pompously, eyed the policeman holding the girl. The policeman's eye was beginning to darken. That seemed to give his honor an idea.

"Then we'll charge you with attempted murder," he said.

The girl gargled, "You—why, you——" She eyed Doc Savage. "Are you going to stand for this?"

"It is hardly my position to interfere with the due courses of the law," Doc Savage told her, without emotion.

She seemed about to jump up and down in her rage.

"What a flat tire you turned out to be!" she cried. "Why, I have heard you could do anything you wanted to. And here you——"

"Take her away," said his honor.

They took her away.

"A rambunctious young woman," his honor said, as he conducted them into the Municipal Office Building.

They met the city attorney, the heads of the police department and some others in the mayor's private office. The held a conference. Doc heard how the earth tremors had first been noticed about three weeks previously, and listened to a description of the roaring sound which different persons had heard.

There were other details, which he already had heard. As far as developing something new was concerned, the conference was a dud.

"How about our irascible feminine colleague?"

Johnny asked when he and the bronze man were apart.

"The girl?" Doc queried. "Let her sit it out."

"You're a woman-hater, are you not?" Johnny chuckled.

The bronze man did not commit himself on that.

"This one has too much vinegar and bubbles," he said. "She may be trying to make fools of us."

Johnny squinted. "Can you not tell?"

"No," Doc admitted frankly. "Are you ready to go into the mountains?"

"Into the mountains?" Johnny seemed surprised.

"The earth shocks," Doc said. "We must find exactly what they are. The simplest method of doing that is to spot automatic recording seismographs at scattered points, so that, if there is another shock, we will have something concrete to go on."

"Very well," Johnny said. "I brought the necessary appurtenances for such a project. Any thing else you think I should do?"

"Just keep your eyes open," Doc said. "We want Renny. We want Monk and Ham. They come first."

"Emphatically," Johnny agreed, and departed.

Doc Savage went into the Municipal Office Building, looking for Mayor Leland Ricketts. There was no sign of his honor. Doc made inquiries.

"He departed in a great hurry," some one explained. "I think he got a note."

"Where does he live?" Doc asked.

"On the hill. The rustic type place. You can't miss it."

"Thank you," Doc said.

The rustic type place would have been hard to miss. It was one of the most pretentious log structures Doc Savage had ever seen, more of a mansion than a woodland type home. A young forest must have been denuded in the making of it. Everything about it and all the fittings possible seemed to have been made out of logs.

There was a swimming pool. Or maybe it was a small lake. Probably both, for there was a springboard, a sand beach and a pair of canoes drawn up

on one side. The lake, or pool, at one end was lined
with logs, either natural, or made of concrete and
colored in imitation.

There was a lot of shaggy shrubbery.

Mayor Leland Ricketts over the telephone to
New York had been pompous and friendly. There
might have been some one listening to him. Mayor
Ricketts here in Powertown had been pompous and
not so friendly.

Doc Savage entered the grounds through the
shrubbery, and he did his absolute best to keep from
being seen. He made a complete circuit of the place.
It was as quiet as a tomb.

Doc Savage stood up and walked to the door. He
was not exactly taking a chance. He wore a bulletproof coat under his clothing, and a pair of chain-
mail shorts.

Some one might shoot him in the head, but they
would have to do it accurately, because the bronze
hair in view was not his own, but artificial hair on a
thin but immensely strong metal skullcap. And he was
keeping his eyes open.

A gnarled limb with a knot on the end had been
fashioned into a knocker. Doc Savage stood to one
side of the door, where no one would ordinarily stand,
lifted the knocker and let it fall.

His features wore no particular expression as he
manipulated the knocker, and a bystander could not
have told whether he really expected trouble, or even
a response to his summons.

Doc's features rarely showed emotion. If the
knocker had been a trick machine gun trigger and the
weapon had ripped out, it was doubtful if he would
have shown great wonder.

But he looked astounded at what did happen
when the knocker fell.

There was simply no sound.

The bronze man reacted as if dynamite had
exploded under him. He whipped off the porch and
down back of the nearest shrub. He crushed part of
the bush in landing, and it shook itself back in place

after it was released. The movement made no sound. Doc's impact with the ground had made no sound.

The bright, sunshiny world had become as devoid of sound as the deepest tomb.

It was incredible! It brought that scalp tingling which men mistake for their hair trying to stand on end.

Doc Savage, lying face down, felt a sensation as if small birds were alighting on his back. He turned his head, looking up. Pieces of bark and bits of wood were landing on his back. They came out of the cabin walls. Round holes and splintered places were appearing in the cabin wall.

Judging from their frequency of arrival, the bullets must be coming from a machine gun.

When the bush began to fall apart, Doc Savage crawled. He made no bid for silence. There was no such thing as sound. He did not crawl back into the ground. The shooting was out there somewhere.

He saw a basement window, knocked the glass out of the frame, and cut himself a little as he crawled through. While he had hold of the window sill, there was a faint vibratory tickling in his palms. That was the vibration set up by the impact of the bullets.

Doc Savage, intending to get into the upper regions of the house and look out from some vantage point and identify the gunners, if possible, walked toward the stairway.

The house was a labyrinth of rooms. Doc went through four or five before he sighted a stairway. He went cautiously, using his flake-gold eyes. In the room next to the stairway, there was something which halted him.

Sunlight slanted in through the windows, and there was enough dust in the air to make one of those gray fog bars which are common to sunbeams slanting into rooms. These had been in the other rooms. Doc had studied them carefully. Persons in fast motion stir up the air in a room, and it swirls, at least for a few moments after they are gone. The dust in the other rooms had been still.

In this room, it was in motion.

Doc studied the phenomenon. The movement was close to the floor, and the window was near a closed door. Doc Savage went over and tried the door. It was locked. It did not look strong. He yanked—and the door broke open.

Retta Kenn's breath, coming through the crack at the bottom of the door, had been stirring the dust.

The door opened into a closet, and she had been bound securely with lengths of wire which must have come from a floor lamp. She looked as if she had been in a fight, for she was scratched, her hair was tousled, and something—a blow, no doubt—had started her nose swelling.

"I thought you were in jail," Doc Savage told her.

He heard himself, but it was only because of such vibration as the vocal cords transmitted through the bony structure of his head to the ear mechanism.

"Turn me loose," the girl said.

Her voice made no sound, but Doc Savage understood her words because he was an experienced lip reader.

He shook his head, as if he had no idea what she had said. It was not exactly bald deceit. He could have shook his head thus for any one of many reasons.

He took the wire off her ankles, stood her up, turned her and began loosening her wrists from behind her. She had not noticed that he had stood her so that he could watch her features in the mirror on top of a chiffonier.

She was excited and she said something to herself. She said it so rapidly that he all but missed it, and he made a mental resolution to brush up on his lip reading, even as he caught it.

"Watch your step, old girl," she said. "You're going to have to explain why you were out here, and make it sound good."

She must have been talking to herself.

Doc Savage got her loose, and guided her toward the upper regions of the house. Suddenly he could hear their footsteps, the ticking of clocks in various parts of the house. There seemed to be scores of clocks. He had not noticed them particularly before, but now he noted that they were on every wall. The mysterious silence had come to an end.

"Ha!" said the girl. "They've shut it off."

"What off?"

She twisted around and looked at him. "The thing that stops all sound, whatever it is."

"So it is a machine," he said.

"How do I know," she snapped. "It would have to be, wouldn't it?"

Doc Savage did not answer. He had found a second-story window—a part only of the big log house jutted up to a second story—and was looking out. He could see no one. The vicinity looked utterly peaceful. Such birds as he could see in the shrubbery did not look excited.

"I thought you were in jail," he told the girl.

"What a help you turned out to be," she snapped. "Why did you let them lock me up?"

"You were safer there," he told her. "This is no affair for a woman. Men are getting killed. How did you get out?"

She sniffed, as if his opinion on that point were not worth considering. Then she answered the question about the jail.

"I stumbled and fell down," she said. "The very polite policeman bent over to pick me up, and I kicked his head. He went to sleep and I walked out."

"Very unwise," Doc said. "Now they'll put you in jail and really keep you there."

She said in an ominous voice, "I wasn't safe in jail. My life was in danger."

"Why?"

She made her voice even more ominous.

"Mayor Leland Ricketts is the Roar Devil," she said.

"You have proof?" Doc Savage asked.

"I have," she said.

Chapter XII

THE WRONGED INVENTOR

Doc Savage heard a commotion among the birds outside. It was around to the west of the house, and he hurriedly found a window facing in that direction. It was only a hawk.

"Is it a secret, how you got in that closet?" he asked.

Retta Kenn had found a mirror-door in the room and was frowning at herself.

"Am I a sight," she said. "No, it's not a secret. You see, I told you V. Venable suspected his honor——"

"Why?"

"I told you I didn't know why," she snapped. "Don't interrupt. I came out here to see what I could find. Believe it or not, I did look around for you first, but you were in the Municipal Office Building, and I couldn't come in there, because that's where they have their jail and the police station and all the rest. So I came out here and got in the house and had bad luck. The Roar Devil caught me."

"Mayor Ricketts?" Doc corrected questioningly.

"Well, Mayor Ricketts, then," she said grudgingly. "He grabbed me and we had a fight. The old boy can scrap. He tied me up. All of the time, he kept looking out the windows real anxiouslike. He seemed to be expecting some one or something."

"Is that all?"

"That's all."

"I thought you said you had proof that Mayor Ricketts was the Roar Devil," Doc told her.

"That proves it as far as I am concerned." She looked at the bronze man closely, inquisitively. "Don't you think he acted queer? And where did he go?"

Doc Savage did not answer that. He said, "We will look his establishment over."

They began to search the big log mansion. It was no small job. There must have been at least fifty rooms, and none of them small. There should have been numerous servants for such a menage. They encountered none.

"Where's all the help?" the girl puzzled aloud.

It was Doc Savage who turned up the first really interesting item. This was a closet in a remote part of the attic, and the door was padlocked. Doc Savage picked the lock with a special tool which he carried for that purpose.

Guns were inside the closet. There were rifles, revolvers and three submachine guns, along with some thousands of rounds of ammunition.

The girl indicated the machine guns and said, "Uncle Sam don't allow this."

"Unless the possessors have permits," Doc corrected.

They did not search steadily, but kept a sharp lookout through the windows. They saw nothing alarming.

"Why didn't you go out and hunt the gunners?" the girl asked.

"Chances are one in a thousand of catching them," the bronze man told her. "Wise crooks have cars handy. These ones, from their previous actions, seem to be wise. Anyway, Mayor Ricketts is the chief interest at present."

In what seemed to be his honor's study, they scrutinized papers. There were numerous rent receipts, and Doc examined those hurriedly. Ricketts seemed to own considerable property.

The girl was going through the wastebasket.

"Come here," she said suddenly.

Doc went over. She had pieced together a torn paper. There was typing on it, but the typing was hardly readable at the end; the typewriter ribbon must have stuck. It was as if some one had been writing a note, had made a botched job of it, and had discarded this sheet for another try.

They studied the note closely and finally managed to read it. There was no address on it.

> Doc Savage's man Renny in Powertown.
> Trail him and get him.
> > The Roar Devil.

Doc Savage put another sheet of paper in Mayor Leland Ricketts's typewriter and repeated the message. He compared the typing. The letter "Y" stuck high on both. He wound the typewriter ribbon. There was a hole in one end where the ribbon had stuck and the keys had beaten it.

"Now, who do you think is the Roar Devil?" Retta Kenn asked with elaborate sarcasm.

Doc Savage looked at her closely. "You did not by chance have that note with you?"

For a moment, she looked as if she were going to blow up. Then she shrugged and hissed disgustedly.

"Oh, sure," she said with elaborate scorn. "I had those machine guns upstairs in my pocket, too. I tied myself up and——"

Her voice stopped. Her lips still moved. No sound came. Doc snapped his fingers. He could not hear the snap.

He whipped to a window, looked out. Men were running through the shrubbery toward the house. They wore conventional bulletproof vests, steel military helmets, and they carried auto rifles and machine guns.

The bronze man vaulted a chair on his way to the door. It was the front door, and it was open. The door itself leaned drunkenly and part of the jamb had been shot away in the previous attack.

Doc Savage produced a rather plump metal case. The interior was plush lined, with numerous small pockets, and in these reposed what at first might have been mistaken for glass marbles. They were thin glass globes filled with a bilious-appearing liquid.

Doc lifted one out, handling it with great care, and flung it as far as it could toward the attackers. He followed with a second. Then he backed from the door.

A moment later, a storm of bullets came in.

Lead was striking the house. The vibration told that. A metal vase, hit by a bullet, went skipping across the floor. Glass fell out of windows. There was absolutely no sound.

Doc Savage ran to the rear of the house. Men were coming there, attacking. Like those in front, they were equipped to almost military completeness.

The bronze man threw two of his glass bulbs. They broke in front of the attackers. He did not wait to see results, but spun, got the girl, Retta Kenn, and urged her up the stairs. He did not stop at the second floor. He went on, clambering into the attic and up into a tiny cupola.

It seemed to be the bronze man's desire to get as high above the ground as possible.

The cupola had small windows—slits, rather— through which they could look out. The girl stared at the attackers. Some—those nearest the house—had gone down. She turned to Doc. Her lips framed a word.

"Gas."

He nodded.

"But they may have masks," her lips formed.

Doc nodded, then shrugged as if it did not make any difference. He managed to convey his opinions without words almost as clearly as he could have with them.

The girl looked out again. The men to the rear had put on masks. They raced forward. They got almost to the house. Then they began falling. The wise ones turned, and some of them managed to run to safety before they fell.

The girl turned to Doc Savage. "The masks do not seem to help them."

He made a gesture which indicated that it did not matter.

"What kind of gas is it?" she asked.

His hands, his shoulders, his features moved. Although he did not speak a word, it became perfectly clear that the gas was one which went through the pores of the skin, and that the only effective protection against it was a suit which covered the body completely and would keep it out.

"It looks like we've got them," she lipped.

The attackers had come to the conclusion that they had caught a Tartar, and instead of trying to take the house, were now endeavoring to assist those who had been overcome and get away from the vicinity. It became evident that they were going to succeed.

If Doc Savage had any idea of preventing them from getting away, it was made hopeless by the stream of bullets which other men farther away kept pouring at the log mansion. A small torrent of slugs marched over the cupola, and Doc and the girl sought safety below.

They waited there for some minutes. It was foolish to show themselves. There was death everywhere around the house.

Then, suddenly, they could hear again.

The girl spoke first.

"After the first attempt, they waited, thinking we would try to come out," she said. "When we did not appear, they decided to rush the place. They have probably gone now."

Doc Savage said, "That is what I thought."

She stared at him. "But you told me they had probably gotten away in cars——" She shook her head. "You're a strange one. I'm beginning to get scared of you."

She did not sound scared. She sounded quite cheerful, as if she were enjoying herself hugely.

Doc Savage looked out. Men were gone from the grounds. They had succeeded in taking away all who had been overcome by the gas.

"Let's go down," the girl suggested. "Maybe we'll find one of them. We could ask him some questions."

"Not yet," Doc told her. "That gas is a new type. It is heavy, and hangs close to the earth. It is moved by the wind, but slowly. We will have to wait until it is carried off."

At the end of fifteen minutes the bronze man indicated that it might be safe, and they went down. They went out to the street—or road, for the town was some distance away—and found no sign of their enemies.

"We will look the grounds over," Doc decided. "Footprints, and that sort of thing."

They found footprints. The ground was soft, and it had been trampled wildly. Many of the prints were as clearly defined as could be wished. Doc Savage merely looked at them.

"Aren't you going to measure them or photograph them, or something?" the girl asked.

He said he wasn't.

"Why not?"

He said that he would recognize any one of them if he saw it again, saying it casually, as if it were nothing out of the ordinary. She stared at him.

"Bless me!" she gulped. "I believe you mean it? What are you—the original camera eye?"

He did not explain that it had taken him years of intensive training and study and practice to develop such extraordinary abilities as he had. He went on examining the grounds.

They neared the big swimming pool and the girl let out a gasp.

"Look!" she pointed. "A dead man!"

The man lay on his back, his body twisted grotesquely, and his head was as wet and soggy as a sponge soaked in red ink; but he was not dead.

Beside him was an ornamental sun dial which looked like a log, but which was concrete painted to resemble a log. The man's head had come into contact with that, for some of his hair was sticking to the jagged imitation bark.

They looked at him; he was breathing noisily. He was a gaunt man, and he needed a shave, clean clothes, a haircut, a bath. He looked more like a bum than a real bum, almost as if he had made up for the part.

Doc Savage leaned over and did several things to him. The things he did showed the man was genuinely unconscious. One faking senselessness would have reacted differently.

The swimming pool was only a few yards away. Doc Savage went to it. The water seemed very deep at this point, and he was careful as he swung down and soaked a handkerchief. He came back and bathed the victim's face. The bronze man always carried a small emergency kit, and he used the smelling salts from that.

The trampish-looking man reacted to the salts, but not as much as he should have. Doc was feeling for traces of skull fracture when the fellow showed that he had come to more completely than he had let on.

He slashed a furious blow at Doc's jaw. Doc moved enough to let the fist go by, as if he had expected just that. The man grabbed him. He let the fellow take hold. Then he grasped the fellow's wrists, brought them together and held them easily with one hand.

The man gave up.

"All right," he snarled. "Take me back to the Roar Devil."

A slight stiltedness in the man's speech made Doc believe he was not native born.

Doc Savage studied him. "You know me?"

The man glared. "I do not. You must be a new member of the gang."

"I am Doc Savage," Doc said.

"*Sacre!*" The man swallowed several times, as if to keep genuine amazement down. "You are the terrible one of whom they are so frightened! What luck I have to fall into your hands!"

Doc asked, "How did you get here?"

"They have me a prisoner," the man said eagerly.

"I am with them, in their power, at a hiding place they use. Where it is, I do not know. But a call did come from their leader, the Roar Devil, telling them they must come in the great hurry and protect his house."

"The Roar Devil's house?"

"That is right. They bring me with them, and come to guard this house, and they try to shoot somebody. I do not know who, but maybe it is you, no?"

"It was," Doc agreed.

"They have it the bad luck the first time," the man went on, taking some liberties with his grammatical construction. "They wait for you to come out, but you fool them, so they try it once more, and something happen. There is the much excitement. I break away but the bad luck I have. I am run, oh, so fast, when I fall down and bump my head on that——"

He pointed at the sun dial, swore at it, looked at the girl and apologized.

"Who are you?" Doc asked.

"Flagler D'Aughtell," said the disreputable-looking man.

Retta Kenn started and gasped, "Oh! Then you are the inventor who has a cabin in the mountains—a sort of laboratory and home?"

"I thought they burned it down," said D'Aughtell. "They told me they had."

"And you had an assistant named Mort Collins?" the girl continued.

"*Had* is correct," D'Aughtell muttered sorrowfully. "They killed him."

"No!" the girl corrected. "He was drugged or something, as they did those two engineers. I saw him in the cabin."

"They killed him later," D'Aughtell told her. "They got worried and went back and got him and shot him to death. They have his body in their hiding place."

"They have held you a prisoner?" Doc asked.

Again D'Aughtell nodded gloomily.

"It is a horrible existence I have led," he said.

"They make the raid on my cabin, and take me away. They also steal much of my scientific equipment, and smash the rest. Their chief, this Roar Devil, is a scientific fiend. He is mad over science."

"Why did they keep you alive," Doc asked.

"To make them a powerful explosive," D'Aughtell growled. "It is a common explosive they want, trinitrotoluene. They have the ingredients. Me, they make mix it. I have to do so. I do not want to die."

"What were they using if for?" Doc queried.

"That, I do not know," the other declared. "They are use great quantity of it, however."

Then he shut his eyes tightly, sighed, and a pallor overspread his face. He slumped on the ground.

"Fainted," the girl said.

They telephone for a taxicab, and D'Aughtell had not revived by the time the machine got there. Doc Savage loaded the senseless man into the cab, got in with the girl and directed the hackman to take them to the airport.

He did not tell the cab driver anything, nor did the latter seem to notice anything strange about Mayor Leland Ricketts's log mansion. They had met him in the driveway, so that he had not come close enough to notice the marks left by bullets.

They were halfway to the airport when the earth gave a distinct lurch under the car, and the driver, probably more because of fright than because the machine had been thrown out of control, ran into a ditch but did no damage.

Dust jumped up from the roadway. A chimney fell over on a near-by house. There was only the one shock.

The taxi driver said in a horrified voice, "My wife and kids are in a house below that dam!"

They all listened. There was no rumbling to show that the big dam had broken.

"Drive on to the airport," Doc directed.

To their ears came the thump of an explosion from a considerable distance away. A person with experience could have told that the blast was one of considerable magnitude.

The driver was frightened. Although there had been no earth shock, he stopped the car again and listened, horror on his face. Finally, after he had stared fearfully for some time in the direction of the great dam, he got back in and drove on.

"I wonder what that was," Retta Kenn pondered aloud.

She sounded as if she were enjoying the whole thing.

Chapter XIII

ONE BY ONE

When Doc and the girl arrived at the airport, Doc found his plane nearly entirely destroyed.

The tires had survived; that was strange, but then powerful explosives often do the unusual. The rest of the plane was a ruin, with a second look necessary to even tell what it had been.

It bore no resemblance to the costly and extremely modern speed plane in which Doc Savage and Johnny had come to Powertown from New York.

The man in charge of the airport explained.

"It must've been a bomb that somebody put in when nobody was looking," he said. "We didn't see a soul around before the thing went off, and not after, either."

Doc Savage went back and got in the taxicab.

"So this is the explosion we heard," the driver mumbled.

Retta Kenn tapped D'Aughtell, who was still unconscious, and assumed a knowing expression.

"Some of the trinitrotoluene he said he was forced to mix," she said. "But why blow up your plane?"

"Keep me from spying on them from the air," the bronze man said. "Maybe they knew that ship was fitted with marvelous air photographic equipment—cameras that could take almost microscopic pictures of the ground. And maybe they just did it to get my goat."

He directed the taxicab to the local express station, and sat without moving or speaking, but watching D'Aughtell steadily, until he got out at the station to ask for a box which might have come in from New York addressed to Alexander Smithers.

The express agent looked, and came back with Alexander Smithers's box. Doc produced a driver's license which proved to the agent's satisfaction that he was Alexander Smithers.

The box was large and of metal, and when Doc Savage opened it, proved to hold, among other things, a radio transmitter-and-receiver of unusual compactness.

"There was one in the plane," he explained. "I sent this one up from New York before we left, just on the chance that there might be an emergency."

He did not add that much of his phenomenal success was due to that simple habit of preparing well in advance, against every conceivable emergency. He probably prepared for a hundred things that never happened for every one that did.

Johnny was waiting on the air when Doc tuned in and attempted reaching him. Johnny had carried a portable transmitter-and-receiver with him.

"What did your seismographs show on that last earth tremor?" Doc Savage asked him.

"Something that wasn't very nice," Johnny said with small, gloomy words.

The fact that he continued to use small words showed that the gaunt archæologist and geologist was worried. He began to speak slowly and distinctly over the air, and Doc Savage did not interrupt the recital. It was not necessary. Johnny started out supplying even the minute details.

"I went to the region which seems central in the disturbances," Johnny said. "I took a car, then walked. I went alone, carrying my equipment, which consisted of four of those supersensitive recording seismographs and a sonic apparatus for ascertaining in some degree the nature of the strata underlying the vicinity.

"I set up my instruments nine miles north of Powertown, and two miles west. You will recognize the spot by the large mountain, which is very dark and seems composed entirely of stone. The mountain is rugged, marked with many ravines and pits, and there are very few trees on it.

"I took sonic tests of the underlying strata and found something rather peculiar and as things are turning out, quite ominous. For instance——"

There was a pause—deep silence.

"For instance what?" Doc asked.

"Help!" Johnny's voice screamed out of the speaker.

The other transmitter banged as if some one had kicked it. Then its carrier wave went off the air.

Doc Savage sat perfectly motionless before his own receiver, listening for a long time. He did not move a muscle. He was so still that the girl, Retta Kenn, looked at him, and something about his immobility seemed to appall her. For the first time she looked as if she were not enjoying herself.

And then D'Aughtell revived. He groaned several times, turned over, and since he was lying in the taxicab, fell out of the machine. That, instead of putting him out again, revived him more.

Retta Kenn went over to D'Aughtell.

Doc Savage still crouched before his radio receiver. He seemed unaware of anything else.

Retta Kenn asked D'Aughtell, "Have you ever seen the Roar Devil?"

"Yes," said D'Aughtell.

"Who is he?" the girl questioned. Her voice was a snap.

"His name is Ricketts," said D'Aughtell.

"The mayor——"

"Mayor Leland Ricketts of Powertown," said D'Aughtell emphatically.

Doc Savage seemed not to have heard. He had not taken his strange flake-gold eyes from the radio receiver over which Johnny's last words—that cry for help—had come.

Chapter XIV

CANDIDATES FOR DEATH

Johnny looked like a scholar. He was. He also looked like a man who, if given a hard shove, would fall apart. That was a wrong impression. He was as tough as walrus hide, and he knew all of the fighting tricks, either under the Queensbury or the dock-walloper rules.

He had been fighting for five minutes. He was not doing so badly.

A man snarled and jumped at Johnny's throat with both hands held out like claws. Johnny stuck the two forefingers of his right hand in the man's eyes, and the man fell back and rolled over and over, cursing and yelling at his companions to kill Johnny and cut his heart out.

There was seven of the attackers, all of them gentlemen who would have looked out of place in a drawing-room. They had started the thing quite confidently. They were not so sure of themselves now.

Three of them were senseless. The one just blinded was the fourth.

The three survivors cursed and grunted and gasped and kicked and slugged. They were in the wreck of the radio transmitter-and-receiver, which had been trampled to pieces. They were becoming tired. Johnny, on the other hand, seemed just warming up.

"Bony—buzzard!" one gasped.

Johnny performed the painfully unexpected feat of kicking a man behind him in the face without turning around, and the fracas came to a momentary pause.

"We're gonna have to croak—him—after all!" a man panted. "Chief said—do that—if we had to!"

Johnny had been wondering about that. The men had guns, but they had not tried to use them. In the back of Johnny's mind was the intention of fighting as long as they seemed inclined to keep it up without bringing in guns.

One of the men dragged out an automatic. Johnny promptly stopped fighting. He half expected to be shot. But his foes appeared glad enough to have him stop.

"Shoulda thought of the gun before," one grunted.

Johnny panted loudly. He carefully made his arms tremble and his knees go rubbery.

"Played himself out," chuckled one of the men. "But man, he sure surprised me!"

Johnny sat down. He looked as if he had collapsed. If any one noted he had come down on a smooth hard rock, they did not think anything peculiar about it.

Nor did any one seem to notice that Johnny had torn a button off the cuff of his coat and was surreptitiously making marks on the flat stone. The rock was hard. Johnny's secretive scrapings on it left no perceptible trace.

The men gathered around him after they had rested a bit, searched him, and took away his machine pistol, ammo drums, money, notebooks, seismograph charts, and other paraphernalia.

"What'd you learn about the whole thing?" one of the men asked Johnny. "Get the low-down?"

"Certain bicephalous, consanguineous eventualities," Johnny said, without batting an eye.

The listeners looked slightly dizzy.

"We've heard about them words," one said. "They sure live up to advance notices!"

They proceeded to revive their companions—no one had been damaged seriously—and get them in moving condition. Johnny watched them.

A small stream made noisy gurgles near by. It was because of that sound that the assailants had been able to come upon him unawares, Johnny decided. Of course, he had been careless to the extent that he had permitted himself to become too absorbed by what he had been doing. That is a common fault of scholars, or, possibly, not a fault, because it is impossible to learn anything without concentration.

They must have been watching him for some time, Johnny perceived, because they had gathered up the seismographs which he had planted at intervals. They now destroyed these, using stones to beat them into a metal pulp. Johnny winced with each destructive blow. Those things had cost more than the average bank president earns in a year.

"You are the Roar Devil's men?" he demanded.

"Heck, no," said one of the men, acting surprised.

Johnny frowned at him. "You are not going to lie to me?"

"Heck, no," said the other. "We're field agents of Santa Claus. We go around looking for little boys——"

"Stow it!" some one snapped. "This guy was lallygagging over that radio when we jumped him, and somebody is liable to have gotten wise. We'd better blow."

They walked the bed of the noisy little creek. Sometimes the water was up around their hips. More often, it washed their ankles. It was cold. The men shivered and swore.

The creek dropped down into one of the minor reservoirs—minor only in that it was but a part of the development around Powertown. The lake was deep, a mile wide and a number of miles long.

Where the creek emptied into the lake, there was a hidden flat-bottomed boat fitted with an outboard motor. The men got in. They flooded the carburetor of the outboard in trying to start it, and the man with the starting cord accidentally whipped the faces of those behind him with the cord. They nearly fought.

After the motor had started and the boat was moving, it could be seen that the exhaust—the pipe was underwater—was leaving a trail of oil.

"Somebody mixed too much oil in the gasoline," a man gritted. "Wonder if anybody can trail us by that?"

They worried about it, but did not change their course. By the time they reached the other side of the lake, they had hit upon a plan.

They unloaded on a sloping rock beach which would retain no footprints. They did not bring the boat clear in, but waded ashore, then turned the boat and, with the motor wide open, headed it across the lake.

They had been lucky in adjusting the motor for direction, because the boat did not swing much from the course they had intended.

"It'll run upon the beach hard wherever it hits," a man chuckled. "That'll make it look like it was hauled up."

"Come on," another said impatiently. "The big-shot may have gotten in."

It looked like a little summer camp, very peaceful. There was a golf course of nine holes, with several men playing on it. The men were correctly dressed for the game; but they were playing terribly, slicing balls into the rough and missing swings entirely. Some of them were acting as caddies, but their attitudes were strange, because they swore terribly at players who accidentally drove balls into the rough.

There were tennis courts, with lean, hard-looking players on them. There was a swimming pool, and more than one man in swimming or getting a sun-burn had bullet scars on his person.

There were no women in sight.

"The hangout, eh?" Johnny asked.

One of his captors looked disgusted.

"You catch on that quick?" he growled.

"It would not fool a policeman thirty seconds," Johnny replied.

They advanced toward what was ostensibly a small hotel, from which a driveway led toward a distant paved highway. Men, neat in white flannels, had dice and poker games going on the veranda.

Looking them over, Johnny decided they were as hard an aggregation as he had ever observed. They were older than the average mob of criminals, too. Johnny had been through penitentiaries, where he had been struck by the youth of the inmates—the majority of them around twenty. The ages of these men would average between thirty and forty. Whoever had assembled them believed in experienced heads.

No guns were in sight. Probably that was in case the police should pay a visit.

Johnny was escorted inside. The lobby was large and ornate, and there was a fountain and a pool in which fish swam. The pool was quite large.

They led him to the fountain. He noted that a small imitation brook, fish swimming in it, ran off across the lobby floor, and was crossed by tiny rustic bridges. It was rather clever.

One of the men pointed at the pool and said, "In!"

Johnny eyed the pool. It was deeper than he had expected, but clear, and he could see the long green strands of artificial moss in the bottom. There was moss on the sides, but the pool looked what it was supposed to be.

"Going to drown me here?" Johnny asked. "Rather preternatural, no?"

He was given a shove and fell into the pool with a great splash. Because his hands were still bound, Johnny knew he would have to clamber up the sides to get out, so, while he was still under, he stroked with his feet, shoving himself over.

To his astonishment, he came up under a hidden lip beyond the moss, and found himself in an air space. The nature of the pool must be cleverly camouflaged with the moss, and mirrors, as well.

Hands reached down and seized him. He was hauled, dripping, into a space that was very cramped. Then he was dragged down what seemed to be a ladder, for he banged its rungs in falling and was kicked by his captor. He was stood erect in a narrow passage and marched forward, then down steep steps and into a brightly lighted room. The lights were so bright that he could not see for a moment.

Monk's small, childlike voice said, "Well, do look who is with us!"

Johnny's eyes accustomed themselves quickly to the light, and he could make out Monk, and Ham as well, shackled by chains to concrete rings in the floor.

"A very unceremonious encounter," Johnny said.

"Holy cow!" boomed a voice from a corner. "How'd they get *you?*"

It was Renny, also chained. He was battered, and not many of his clothes were still left on him. The hide was practically all gone from the knuckles of his enormous hands.

Johnny explained how he had been captured. He was not interrupted, except that his captors equipped him with another chain and fastened him to the floor. They did not, however, try to stop his speech.

"Have you gentlemen learned the motivation of our fond hosts?" he finished questioningly.

Renny shrugged; Monk shook his head, and Ham stared gloomily.

"The trouble seems to be between the Roar Devil and Dove Zachies," Renny said, booming. "Dove Zachies has something hidden that he is determined the Roar Devil shall not have, and the Roar Devil is just as determined to get it."

"Know what it is?" Monk asked Johnny.

"No. Don't you?"

"Nary a guess," Monk grumbled. "We been putting together all we heard, and we about half concluded whatever it is ain't money."

"Then what could it be?"

"Your guess is as good as anybody's," Monk told him.

Ham studied Johnny intently. "You were up here with those seismographs and things when the earth gave one of its shimmies. What did you decide?"

"I decided that things are very bad, and can become worse," Johnny said slowly, shunning his usual big words. "I will explain why. My soundings with the sonic apparatus showed me an enormous earth fault of rather unusual formation. For instance, some hundreds of feet below the surface the so-called bedrock is interrupted by a strata of sand and gravel which, in turn, lies on other bedrock.

"This sand and gravel sheet slopes upward at an angle, and you might liken it to a layer of ball bearings under the surface of the earth. In other words, every pronounced shock causes a correspondingly much greater shift in the earth surface.

"For instance, I am quite sure that the surface of the region around Powertown, and especially about the dams, has moved some twelve or fifteen feet recently. You can guess what effect that has on the surface. It has resulted in the breaking of dams, and it will result in the breaking of others if more blasts are set off."

"Blasts!" Monk interjected. "What are you driving at?"

"The thing which causes the earth shocks, as far as the seismographs showed, and they are very dependable, is an explosion of tremendous power," said Johnny.

"Nerts!" Monk said. "An explosion big enough to cause the surface of the earth to slide would be heard for miles."

"You forget," Johnny said, "the silencing device, or whatever it is that brings those periods of absolute silence."

"That Roar Devil is a clever cuss," Monk grunted.

"If we only knew who he is," Johnny murmured.

Monk blinked. "We do."

"You mean——" Johnny gulped, and seemed too surprised to continue.

"Oh, we've overheard enough to tell us who he is," Monk said.

"Who is he?"

"Mayor Leland Ricketts, of Powertown," Monk said.

There was a commotion at the entrance. The guard looked up the passage, then grinned over his shoulder at the prisoners picketed out on the floor.

"You've got company coming."

There was more scuffling, then a man was hauled through the opening, kicked ungently to the center of the floor, and staked out with one of the chains and iron rings.

Johnny stared at the newcomer. It was V. Venable Mear.

"So you're back with us," Monk told V. Venable Mear amiably.

That seemed to indicate Mear had been a previous companion. Johnny asked about this, and was assured it was true—that V. Venable Mear had been hauled away, some hours before.

"They seemed to think I might know how they could catch Dove Zachies," Mear explained. "They have had me in a room firing questions at me since."

Johnny continued to study V. Venable Mear, as if to convince himself of the man's exact position in the mysterious trend of events.

"One might say you are a private detective," Johnny said abruptly.

"A criminal psychologist," V. Venable Mear corrected; then he reconsidered. "Maybe private detective is a general term which would describe my present connection with this affair, if one did not want to be too specific."

"And you were hired by a mysterious individual known as April Fifth?"

"Correct."

"Who is April Fifth?"

"I have not the slightest idea," V. Venable Mear registered curiosity. "How did you learn all of this?"

"Retta Kenn told us."

"An estimable young lady. I am glad you learned what you did. I fear you suspected me of being the Roar Devil."

Johnny did not admit or deny this, but nodded at V. Venable Mear. "You seemed to have been shot during the raid on your house in New York."

For answer, Mear opened his shirt. His shoulder was in bandages.

"Does that satisfy you?" he asked.

Renny boomed, "Lay off! Didn't we tell you Mayor Leland Ricketts is the Roar Devil."

A man in the door laughed, and said, "I hope your boss, Doc Savage, is as sure of that as you are."

Monk looked at the man, who was one of the Roar Devil's gang.

"Better not wish that, guy," he said. "Doc might find a way to gloom onto your chief."

The other sneered. "Get wise to yourself, monkey knuckles."

"Wise?" Monk frowned.

"Sure," chuckled the other. "We've been taking you for a ride. The Roar Devil is not Mayor Ricketts. We've been kidding you!"

Chapter XV

THE BREAK

Silence followed the announcement that the Roar Devil was not His Honor, Mayor Ricketts of Powertown. Monk, Ham and Renny seemed rather firmly convinced on the point, probably due to what they had heard in the past. Johnny held his peace because he did not have enough information to hold any convictions in any direction.

V. Venable Mear was quiet because he did not seem to feel good. Once or twice, when he moved, he grimaced violently and felt of his body tenderly, as if he had some bad bruises.

Unexpectedly, Johnny spoke. His words were not English, but a queer, low, not unmusical guttural language.

V. Venable Mear eyed them. "I believe that was the Mayan dialect, was it not?"

He was right. Johnny, Monk, Ham and Renny nearly fell over. It was the first time in the so-called civilized world that they had ever encountered a man who even knew what the language was, although they were aware that there must be some.

The tongue was that of a lost race, the mighty ruling clan of the ancient Mayan empire, a people lost for centuries. Doc Savage and his men often spoke this Mayan tongue when they did not wish to be understood.

"You understand Mayan?" Johnny demanded of V. Venable Mear.

"Not that Mayan," Mear said. "I was in Yucatan, and learned one of the modern dialects."

"I'll speak that, then," Johnny said.

The gaunt archæologist and geologist then launched into the slurring syllables of the modern Mayan dialect, with which he and his companions were also familiar.

"They gave me the usual searching," Johnny said. "They even pried the heels loose from my shoes to see that there was nothing inside. They did not, however, remove the buttons from my coat. The top buttons and the bottom buttons, if crushed together, will burst into flame, giving off a gas that will make a man senseless if he breathes it. The gas is merged with the air and rendered harmless after a few seconds, so that you can escape it by holding your breath."

"I know all about that," Monk said. "Doc worked out the formula for the gas, and I helped him. You must shut your eyes, too. The stuff kinda smarts if you don't."

"That guard at the door has the key to these locks," Renny boomed in Mayan. "I am going to raise a fuss, and make him mad enough to come over here and kick me or something. When he is over here, use the gas. That way, we can get to him after he goes down. The way it is, we couldn't reach him on account of these chains."

"Excellent," Johnny agreed.

The bony archæologist and geologist began to work carefully. Without being discovered, he plucked buttons off his coat and carefully crushed them on the concrete floor. It was necessary to have them smashed into a fine powder, he explained quietly in Mayan. He made two piles, which looked no different.

"I'm about ready," he said in Mayan.

Renny opened his mouth to start his yelling, then closed it. The guard came down the stairs, followed by another man. The two of them walked over to V. Venable Mear, put handcuffs on him, then unloosened his chain.

"What—what's up?" V. Venable Mear asked nervously.

"That girl," said one of the men. "She's getting in the big-shot's hair. He wants you to tell him a way of grabbing her."

V. Venable Mear yelled, "I won't!"

"So you think," the other snarled.

They took V. Venable Mear away. He turned at the door and said, "I hope your scheme works." He said it in Mayan, rapidly.

The guard struck him a terrific blow, knocking him up the steps, and snarling, "I'm getting tired of hearing that gobbling and clucking among you guys!"

The prisoners left behind were quiet for a time. They did not exchange words, but it seemed mutually agreed that it might be best to wait a little.

At length, Johnny said in Mayan, "We might as well try it now."

"I'll yell," said Renny.

The big-fisted engineer threw back his head and began to howl. His yells were incredible. They all but tore the place apart. The guard, who had been up the steps a few feet, came clattering down.

"Cut that out!" he gritted.

Renny only bawled the louder.

The guard ran toward them. He did not go to Renny, but to Johnny. And he suddenly kicked the two piles of powdered chemicals apart, scattering them on the floor.

"You guys must think I ain't got eyes," he snapped. "That foreign gobble you were speakin' tipped me off!"

Renny said disgustedly, "Oh, what awful luck!"

But it was not over. Johnny had been crouching on his heels and he straightened suddenly, explosively, and butted the guard in the side. The latter was not taken entirely by surprise, but he did not fathom Johnny's true intention in time.

The guard was knocked back across the floor.

Monk was ready. He received the guard in two furry beams of arms. The guard let out one agonized bleat, then Monk banged him on the floor. They rolled. Monk's chain rattled.

The guard got his gun out and managed to shoot it three times. None of the bullets hit anybody, but the noise sounded like a 16-inch rifle in the chamber. Monk managed to knock the man's head against the concrete floor, so that he became senseless.

Monk fought to get the keys to their shackles.

Feet clattered on the ladder. The shots had brought more of their captors. Two, three, four of them. They came in cursing, and charged.

The keys were on a heavy ring and Monk threw them at the foremost man. He hit the fellow in the face, but it only enraged the man. During the next four or five minutes, they were handled roughly.

Handcuffs were put on their wrists. They were loosened from the chains.

"We're moving you birds," said one of the men. "Things are getting hot. We don't want you found here."

They were led up and pushed, one at a time, into the fountain. Coming up in the pool, they were hauled out, dripping water, and forced to stand in the little artificial brook which ran across the lobby floor. No doubt that was why the brook was there—so that persons coming out of the pool would not drip water on the lobby floor, and thus betray the secret entrance.

The occupants of the fake summer hotel surrounded them. They did not seem to approve of the fact that the prisoners were still alive.

"They're dangerous," a man said. "They oughta be bumped."

"Roar Devil's orders are to keep 'em around," another informed him.

"Why?"

"On account of a very simple reason."

"Yeah?"

"These guys know all about this Doc Savage," the other said grimly. "They can tell us things—things that will help put the grab on the bronze guy."

"They won't talk."

"You bet they will!" the other grunted. "The Roar Devil knows all about truth serum and things like that. They'll talk whether they wanna or not."

It became apparent that some of the men were to accompany the prisoners, while another party was assembling out by the tennis courts. A man appeared, bearing arms from some hiding place, and distributed them to this second party.

The purpose of the second group was apparently a mystery to at least some of those who were to accompany Renny and the other prisoners.

"What're they up to?" a man asked.

"The chief has got a scheme," a man replied. "We've got this Doc Savage thinkin' Mayor Leland Ricketts is the Roar Devil. If we can cinch that idea in the bronze guy's head, then croak Ricketts, we'll have handed the bronze guy a dead cat. He'll think he's got the whole thing wound up, especially after he finds his pals, here, croaked. We'll croak 'em after Ricketts is dead. Then we'll all lay low until the bronze guy goes off the job."

"What about the Dove Zachies angle?"

"Chief is all set to glom Zachies right away," chuckled the other. "Once we get Zachies, everything will be jake."

A man glared at Monk, who was listening intently, and snarled, "Pull in them big ears, you chimpanzee!"

Monk, on the point of making an angry retort, broke forth in a wide grin. A man had come into the lobby leading a small animal by a chain. The man limped, was wary of his charge.

It was the pig, Habeas Corpus. The fellow leading the shote carried a long club, apparently to defend himself. Habeas was grunging angrily and showing vicious-looking tusks.

"Say, are hog bites poison?" the man with the pig demanded.

Almost every one laughed at him. The prisoners were started off.

Monk, walking beside Ham, growled, "So Mayor Leland Ricketts ain't the Roar Devil, after all."

Renny, following them, rumbled, "Lookit, you birds—maybe this talk about Ricketts not being the brains is just a gag to throw us off. Maybe he *is* their chief."

Somebody said, "Put the muffler on that gab, back there!"

There was some excitement as the pig, Habeas, bit some one and the victim demanded the satisfaction of shooting the porker, which seemed only to amuse every one.

It was obvious that the shote had made a hit because of his grotesque appearance and his willingness to fight all of the time. The pig was something with which to pass time.

"My vote goes to Ricketts as being their chief," Monk whispered, a little later.

Ham frowned at him much as a teacher would at a distressingly ignorant scholar.

"Haven't you caught on yet who the Roar Devil is?" he asked.

Monk scowled. "Have you?"

"Yes," said Ham. "I am absolutely positive."

Monk continued scowling, then appeared to decide that Ham was trying to rib him, for he affected disinterest and changed the subject.

"I wonder," he pondered aloud, "what Doc is doing?"

Chapter XVI

THE UNSUCCESSFUL SURRENDER

Doc Savage, at that particular moment, was being roundly criticized. This was unusual. He had not been criticized for a long time, because, to most individuals, his methods were quite amazing and left nothing to be desired.

Retta Kenn seemed to see considerable wrong with the way he was doing things.

"You're going around in circles and not accomplishing anything!" the girl snapped.

Doc Savage pretended not to hear her. He stripped off his coat and wrung it out. It gave up almost a quart of water which ran over the floor of Mayor Leland Ricketts's office in the Powertown Municipal Office Building.

"You're all wet!" the young woman snapped. "Where have you been? What have you been doing?"

Doc Savage took off his vest and wrung that out.

"It's been at least two hours since you heard your man Johnny yell for assistance over the radio," the young woman clipped angrily. "You haven't done a thing about it. Dosen't the welfare of your five assistants mean anything to you?"

"Four," Doc corrected. "The fifth man—Major Thomas J. Roberts, better known as Long Tom—is abroad."

"Well, if he was here, the Roar Devil would have him by now," the young woman said cattily. "And you are the fellows who have half the crooks in the world scared of them. A fine bunch of flat tires you turned out to be!"

"Oh, you give everybody a headache!" Flagler D'Aughtell snapped suddenly.

He was standing in the background, and he had been silent until now.

The girl frowned at him, and asked, "Who pulled your string?"

The Powertown chief of police, a fat man without any hair on top of his head but plenty around the sides, came in.

"We have the entire Powertown police force and the New York State troopers looking for Mayor Leland Ricketts," he said. "So far, no one has seen him."

He went out.

Doc Savage looked at the girl and said, "Have you been taking things into your own hands? I told you not to say anything about Mayor Ricketts."

She sniffed at him.

"And let Ricketts get away scot-free?" she demanded. "Not much! If you're too uppity to accept help from the police, I'm not. How do you know? Maybe a cop might grab Ricketts. Then we'd have the Roar Devil."

"And so you told the police to look for Ricketts, while I was, er—getting wet?" Doc Savage queried.

"Sure," she said. "And you don't seem to like it, and so what?"

Flagler D'Aughtell spoke up again.

"Perhaps we could have her put in jail," he suggested.

"An idea," Doc agreed.

The girl flung back her head and laughed heartily. "I've convinced the chief of police that I'm innocent as the flowers in May."

She seemed very cheerful, as if the more trouble she could stir up, the better she would like it.

Unexpectedly, her face became blank. She stared at the door, her mouth open.

A man had sidled in furtively.

He was a man who had been a fighter once, for there were mounds of gristle about his eyes, and his nose was flat and his ears were not as nature had made them originally. He looked mean, but not stupid.

"Stupe Davin!" exploded the girl.

Doc Savage looked the man over without much evidence of great interest, and said, "I believe you told me Stupe Davin was one of Dove Zachies's men?"

"His bodyguard," snapped the girl. She glared at Davin. "What do you want?"

She took an automatic pistol out of a pocket of her frock and pointed it at "Stupe" Davin.

"Fresh wren!" he scowled at her. "Somebody is gonna push you down plenty before you're through with this!"

Doc Savage said, "You have something on your mind?"

Stupe Davin eyed the bronze man. What he saw seemed to make him uneasy, for he nervously moved his feet and swallowed several times.

"It ain't on my mind," he said. "It's on Dove's."

"Yes?" The bronze man did not seem particularly concerned.

"Dove is scared," said Stupe Davin. "He's scared until he's ready to lay eggs!"

"Unless I am mistaken," the bronze man said, "he has been scared all along."

Davin nodded. "He's worse now. He wants to talk to you."

"What about?"

"A deal." Stupe Davin sounded earnest. "Dove will shoot straight with you this time."

"He couldn't shoot straight with anybody," Retta Kenn put in. "He's too crooked."

"Dry up," growled Stupe Davin. "I'll put my fist down your throat!"

The girl laughed.

Flagler D'Aughtell said nervously, "I don't like this. That Dove Zachies is supposed to be a very clever and unscrupulous crook."

Doc asked Stupe Davin, "You will take us to Dove Zachies?"

"I sure will," gulped Davin.

"All right," Doc said. "We'll go now."

"Count me out!" snapped Retta Kenn. "I'm not entirely crazy!"

"Ditto here," echoed D'Aughtell, fear on his haggard face.

Doc Savage moved—moved more suddenly than it seemed possible he could have. The girl's automatic was unexpectedly in his hand. He pocketed it.

"You are going along," he said, "whether you like it or not."

The girl screamed, "Say, you big cheese! Do you still think I'm a crook?"

"You are going." Doc turned on D'Aughtell. "You can do what you want."

"I'll go," D'Aughtell said promptly. He looked more disreputable, more like a bum, than ever.

"I got a heap waitin' down the street," said burly, ugly Stupe Davin.

They met Dove Zachies in a pleasant little cream cottage in the middle of an apple orchard, the trees of which were in bloom. It was an idyllic little spot, one which hardly looked the part of a gang hideout. But a close observer could have noted that the windows were thick bulletproof glass, the innocent-looking shutters outside were of armor steel, as was the door.

Dove Zachies smiled and bowed, and his bobbing up and down, together with his naturally peaceful appearance, somehow brought the thought of a plump park pigeon being fed corn.

"I am glad to see you," he said earnestly. "Indeed I am. Drink?"

"It might be poisoned," snapped the girl.

Dove Zachies registered disgust in a mild way and inquired, "Was it necessary to bring her along? She gets in my hair."

"She gets in every one's hair," Doc told him. "What is on your mind?"

"I am scared," Dove Zachies said. "This Roar Devil, as you know, caught my men when they were attacking V. Venable Mear's house. Almost my entire organization was in that attack. The Roar Devil got them all. What he did with them, I do not know. I do not think he killed them, but I cannot be sure. At any rate, I am almost alone. These are all I have left."

He waved a deprecating arm to indicate Stupe Davin and half a dozen other vicious-looking gentlemen who had gathered in the room. These gentlemen did not look as if they liked the situation. But there were no guns in sight.

"It was by the rarest good fortune that I did not lead that attack on V. Venable Mear's house," said Dove Zachies. "In which case I would have been taken, and it would all be over."

"Just what is back of this conference?" Doc asked.

"I love my life," Zachies smiled wryly. "You can save it for me. You want the Roar Devil. I can help you get him. We can make a deal."

"I preserve your life, and you help me," Doc replied. "Is that it?"

"A little more than that," Zachies corrected.

"How much more?"

"The Roar Devil is after something of mine," Zachies said. "Something that I have hidden. I must have your word that I am to retain this."

"You mean you want to keep the thing in the cache?"

"Exactly," Zachies agreed. "And you must promise not to try to learn its nature."

"No," Doc Savage stated promptly.

Dove Zachies did not seem surprised.

"Then I and my men will surrender to you," he said. "We give up."

Doc Savage reached in a pocket. He brought out a glass bulb larger than a pigeon egg. He smashed it on the floor. When the bulb broke, a liquid splattered, but evaporated almost instantaneously.

Doc Savage held his breath.

Those in the room—all of them—seemed to go asleep on their feet. They made considerable noise falling to the floor. The girl, near the door, tried to run, but did not get outside before she, too, collapsed.

Doc Savage moved as if he were in no great hurry, and knew exactly what he was doing. He got materials with which to bind them—strips torn from a rug, wires off a clothes line, and adhesive tape from a medicine cabinet. Then he went to work.

When he stood back to survey the job, it was quite evident that Dove Zachies, Stupe Davin and the rest of them would never get free of their own volition.

Retta Kenn was not bound. Neither was Flagler D'Aughtell.

Doc Savage picked the girl and D'Aughtell up and carried them out to the car in which they had come—Stupe Davin's car. He seemed in no particular hurry as he started the motor and drove toward Powertown.

Once he stopped the car and seemed to be thinking deeply. His small trilling sound came out, but in a vagrant sort of way, as if the thing which had provoked it was some conclusion not entirely new, but rather one already fully recognized.

The car was in motion again when the girl and D'Aughtell awakened. They aroused themselves rather quickly, and seemed to suffer no bad effects.

"What was that stuff?" the girl asked.

"An anæsthetic gas," Doc told her. "I have used it for a number of years."

"But didn't it get you?"

"You escape it by holding your breath."

She snapped, "You might have told us."

Flagler D'Aughtell asked, "What about Dove Zachies and what is left of his gang?"

Doc Savage tooled the car around a corner. It was a big machine, quiet and fast. The day had turned out warm. The balmy spring breezes whipped the unbuttoned collar of the bronze man's shirt, but, strangely enough, did not disturb his metallic hair.

"We will tell the police about Zachies," he said finally.

The girl snapped at Doc, "You double-crossed them!" as if he had committed some crime.

"You will distinctly recall that I promised them nothing," he reminded her.

They reached the Powertown police station, and Doc Savage informed the chief that Dove Zachies, who knew much about the mysterious earth tremors menacing the big dam above Powertown, could be found at the cream house in the apple orchard. The police charged off in three squad cars.

Doc, finding them missing when he went back to the car, went hunting the girl and D'Aughtell. He found the girl posing for a newspaper photographer, and located D'Aughtell in the Municipal Office Building lunch room, consuming a sandwich.

"The Roar Devil's men didn't feed me any too well," explained D'Aughtell. "It is hungry like a wolf that I am."

An hour later, the police were back with bad news.

"Dove Zachies and the others were gone!" the chief yelled.

During the next hour, Doc Savage conducted himself as if he had all of the time in the world; indeed, as if there was nothing of particular importance afoot. This aggravated Retta Kenn.

"Your bungling lost us Dove Zachies!" she accused. "You could have brought him and his men back in the car. Why'd you overcome them in the first place? They had surrendered, hadn't they?"

Doc said nothing.

"I think you're a dumb cluck," the young woman said cheerfully.

Doc Savage scowled at her. This was unusual, because he was noted for the degree of calm which he managed to maintain on all occasions. But he was not accustomed to having a young woman around sticking verbal pins into him.

"I did not want Dove Zachies on my hands!" he said sharply.

The young woman looked at him intently, then began to laugh.

"Hah!" she snapped cheerfully. "I thought so! You've got some black, vile plan up your sleeve. But you shouldn't have sent Dove Zachies to his death."

"The Roar Devil will not kill Dove Zachies," Doc told her. "He will make Dove show him where the cache is."

"Ah, the mystery cache," said the young woman. "Now tell me what is in it."

Doc ignored her.

D'Aughtell had been listening, and now he shook his head, got up, and murmured, "This, what is behind this trouble, it is a great mystery to me."

They were in the police chief's office. A box of cigars stood on the chief's desk, open. D'Aughtell walked over, took one of these, found a match, strode to the window and reached up to strike the match on the iron lock of the window. The match popped alight and he brought the flame—*clang!*

Glass fell out of the window. A bullet made a buzz and snap in the room.

D'Aughtell shrieked and fell flat on the floor. A series of agonized moans came from his lips and a scarlet worm came creeping out from under his body.

Chapter XVII

MAYOR RICKETTS

Doc Savage jerked one of the glass anæsthetic bulbs from his pocket and dropped it on the floor, holding his breath as the ball shattered.

The girl, Retta Kenn, taken completely by surprise by the colorless and odorless gas, went to sleep on her feet and fell heavily.

D'Aughtell ceased his moaning and twitching an instant later.

Doc Savage spun through rooms, making for the doorway. There was shouting in some of the rooms, stirred up by the shot. But Doc was out of the building without encountering a cop, or seeing any one.

The Municipal Office Building sat back from the sidewalk, with a strip of grass and shrubbery along the sides. The bronze man got behind an ornamental hedge, followed it to the corner, and ran behind a passing car, across the street.

The driver of the car, not knowing what it was all about and amazed by the apparition of a giant bronze man running beside his machine, completely forgot his handling of the wheel and ran into a telephone pole. The bumper of his car and part of the radiator caved in, and the windshield fell out, after which the motorist got out and began to swear.

Doc Savage went on toward the one spot from which the shot could have come—an automobile dealer's establishment across the street. He did not try to enter the place, but centered efforts on getting a look at the alley behind and the adjacent streets. Doc had moved fast. Unless the gunman had moved with unusual speed, there had not been enough time for him to get away.

There was a man running down a side street away from the automobile dealer's establishment. The man was not running fast, but trotting, rather.

The man had on a checkered sport coat and wore a cap, and there was one of those ample and flashy yellow sport mufflers tied around his neck. His trousers were brown, his shoes brown and white check. He was a bulky man. His dress was that of a sporty summer visitor.

Doc Savage ran after him.

The man in sport clothes saw him. The discovery was made without the fellow turning—he had a small pocket mirror, and he apparently used that to look over his shoulder without swinging, so that his face might be seen.

He began to run more swiftly. And he hurriedly whipped the yellow muffler up so that it covered the lower part of his face. It was obvious that he had previously knotted the muffler to make it just the length for this purpose.

"You!" Doc rapped. "You can't get away!"

The man turned suddenly. He had a gun in his hand; it spouted lead and noise down the street.

Doc Savage sought shelter with more haste than he had intended employing. The other man was shooting from the hip, and there was almost an uncanny accuracy in his marksmanship.

A bullet hit the bronze man almost squarely over the heart, but the bulletproof undergarment which he habitually wore took care of that. Other slugs made ugly sounds close to his ears.

Unexpectedly, a bullet brought Doc down.

Doc controlled his fall, slamming forward so that he landed in the concrete-floored ravine of a driveway which led up into a yard. Without stirring more than necessary, he took stock of the damage.

The lead had come through the chain-mail shorts which he wore to protect his legs down to the knees. The mail was light stuff, in order that it might be worn under his business suit without betraying its presence, and the man down the street was using a foreign automatic which fired a cartridge having almost the characteristics of rifle ammunition.

The bullet had landed a nasty shock, and had torn the flesh some. But it had not put the leg out of commission.

Doc Savage crawled up the driveway, got behind the house and began to run through lawns to head off his quarry. He ran erratically for a while, then got better control over the leg. He caught sight of the man in the sport suit.

The fellow was loping along without any great pretense at haste. He seemed to have the idea that he had stopped pursuit. He looked back often.

He saw Doc Savage. Discovery of the bronze man reacted on the fugitive much as discovery of a hound at his heels would affect a grazing rabbit. He was off like the proverbial shot.

The chase became a wild thing. Doc Savage did not show himself more than necessary. The other man emptied his gun time after time.

They got down into the factory district. There were many big brick buildings, usually with small watchman turrets or booths at the entrances.

Out of one of these turrets, some distance ahead of the fugitive gunman, sprang a uniformed watchman. He was a lean, weather-beaten fellow, and he waved his arms and yelled. There was a gun in one of his hands.

The man in the sport suit snapped a shot at the watchman. It missed. The checkered coat popped around the most convenient corner. He had changed his course, as if to avoid the watchman.

The watchman cursed shrilly, ran to the corner, raised his gun and took a deliberate aim. Reports came from his weapon in a measured volley.

He was shooting down an alley. A gun banged

from the alley in return. The watchman ducked back. He charged his gun with fresh cartridges, stepped out recklessly and fired once. He seemed ready to fire more bullets, but did not. He was standing blowing smoke out of the barrel of his weapon when Doc Savage came up.

"You saw it, gov'nor," he said. "The punk tried to pop me off!"

Doc Savage said nothing, but looked into the alley. A man in a checkered coat, a cap, brown pants, a pair of brown and white check shoes, and with a yellow neck cloth over the lower part of his face, lay in the alley. He was not moving.

"I hope the cops see that it was self-defense," said the watchman.

Doc looked at him. "Was it?"

The other seemed slightly worried. "Well, the guy did shoot at me, but I also chased him, and that might make it look——"

"Forget it," Doc said, and walked down the alley and took a closer look at the man in the sport suit.

One bullet had gone through the checkered cap and the head inside it. There was only the one wound, but that one was enough to have killed instantly.

"Who was he—a hijacker?" demanded the watchman.

Without answering, Doc Savage reached down and stripped the yellow neck cloth from the features of the dead man.

The watchman took one look. He grew white. He seemed about to fall over.

The dead man in the sport suit was Mayor Leland Ricketts, of Powertown.

The watchman seemed to know his honor by sight. He trembled and wiped his forehead. He seemed to be trying to swallow.

"I sure got myself in a crack!" he wailed. "What'm I gonna do?"

"The dead man was trying to kill you, you said," Doc Savage told him.

"Yeah, I know—but, gleeps! A mayor! Croaking a mayor ain't like it was just some ordinary punk who had held up a store or something."

"From all appearances it was perfectly justified," Doc informed him.

The watchman seemed to take heart from that. He speared a cigarette between his lips and ignited it with a shaky hand. The match burned his fingers before he thought to drop it, however. He button-holed Doc Savage eagerly.

"Listen," he gulped. "You stick by me, see? Tell the cops how it was. I got my pistol permit and my license as a special cop, like watchmen get. But this thing of poppin' off a mayor—I'll need all the front I can get. Suppose you put in for me, will you?"

"I will do everything to see that you get justice," Doc Savage told him.

A police siren was caterwauling. The police radio car pulled up, occupied by two officers. One of them stood and swore and asked questions, while the other ran to a telephone and called more officers.

Doc Savage explained what had happened. His word carried weight, it seeemed, for what he said was taken without argument.

The story the girl, Retta Kenn, had told about his honor, Mayor Leland Ricketts, lent weight to Doc Savage's recital.

"Ricketts was this Roar Devil," the police chief said. "There isn't much doubt of it. He tried to croak you, Savage. Must have mistaken D'Aughtell for you in my office at the Municipal Office Building. He shot, saw his mistake, then ran."

"What about me?" the watchmen asked nervously.

"You dictate a statement to the D. A.," directed the policeman. "Then we'll see about getting you your medal."

The watchman had pleasure on his weather-beaten face.

Doc Savage separated a taxi driver from the crowd that had gathered about the scene and had the man take him back to the Municipal Office Building.

Retta Kenn still lay where she had fallen on the floor. Her regular breathing indicated she had not come out from under the effects of the anæsthetic.

Flagler D'Aughtell, the inventor who looked like a bum, was nowhere in sight.

In front of the window where D'Aughtell had fallen after the shot, was a smear of red. Doc Savage was bending over this, studying it with a small but powerful microscope when the girl awakened and sat up.

"You sure do things in a queer manner," she said, sarcastically. "What are you looking for in that pool of blood?"

"It is not blood," Doc Savage told her. "It is ordinary olive oil colored with a red dye."

The girl must have thought she was still suffering from the effects of the gas, and hearing things. She rubbed a hand over her eyes.

"You kidding me?" she demanded.

"D'Aughtell must have had the colored oil in a bottle inside his coat," Doc Savage said. "He broke it, or pulled the cork out, when he fell. He wanted to make it look good."

"I'm getting dizzy!" Retta Kenn gasped. "D'Aughtell was——"

"As crooked as they come," Doc Savage told her. "His acting ability was considerable, too. Had it been necessary to depend only on his conduct to find him out, he might have fooled me."

The young woman got up, went over to the stream of fresh air coming in through the hole that the bullet had made in the window, and took several deep breaths. She turned around and looked at the bronze man.

"I am sure D'Aughtell was just what he pretended to be," she said. "He was an unfortunate inventor whom the Roar Devil had seized and forced to make explosives."

Doc Savage said nothing. He rolled up his trousers leg and began to bandage the slight wound which he had suffered in the chase. It had bled a little.

The girl came over, looking concerned, saw how slight the injury was, sniffed as if she wished it had been something of consequence, and backed away.

"Well!" she snapped. "Aren't you going to argue about D'Aughtell?"

"Your convictions are of no great concern to me," the bronze man told her.

"I could cut your throat," she said, and walked farther away.

It was obvious from her attitude that she intended to have nothing more to say. Doc Savage began talking.

"We found D'Aughtell in the yard of Mayor Ricketts's estate," the bronze man said. "D'Aughtell lay near a sun dial, against which he said he had knocked himself senseless when he fell. That much was the truth, probably."

"I'm not interested in your theories," said the young woman.

Doc Savage went on as if he had not heard her.

"His story about the Roar Devil's men bringing him along when they went to guard Ricketts's home was too thin," he said. "Why should they do that? I went back and dived into the Ricketts swimming pool."

"So that's how you got wet!" the girl interposed.

"In the swimming pool, I found the apparatus which produces those intervals of silence," Doc Savage said. "D'Aughtell was undoubtedly operating it during the attack on Ricketts's house. When I used those gas bombs, he saw the jig was up. The wind must have carried the gas toward him. It was blowing from the house toward the pool.

"D'Aughtell must have gotten scared. He threw his apparatus in the pool, then tried to run away. The gas made him groggy, and he fell and hit the sun dial with his head. When we found him, he trumped up his story to throw suspicion from himself."

The girl seemed, for some reason or other, to find that a sizable and unpleasant pill to down. She stared at the bronze man, made angry faces at him, and seemed not to know what to do next.

"You might have told me!" she snapped. "What kind of a thingamabob was that contraption you found in the swimming pool?"

"It had been smashed to pieces," Doc Savage told her. "No doubt D'Aughtell did that before putting it in the pool, in order that no one finding it might be able to tell how it worked."

"Then you don't know what it is yet?"

The bronze man did not answer that. He seemed entirely concerned with bandaging his leg.

"You give me a pain," she told him.

Doc Savage finished giving first-aid to himself, dropped his trousers leg, stood up and was testing the leg before the young woman seemed to think of something else to say.

"What happened to the man who shot D'Aughtell?" she asked.

"D'Aughtell wasn't shot," Doc told her.

"All right," she said sharply. "There was a shot. A gun went off. What happened to whoever made the gun go off?"

Doc Savage told her about the chase and its termination. He told her exactly what he had seen, and no more.

"And when I took the yellow muffler off the dead man's face, it was Mayor Leland Ricketts," he said in finishing.

Retta Kenn looked cheerful, and vastly relieved. She made a gesture of throwing things off her shoulders.

"So that's that," she said. "The Roar Devil is dead."

"No," Doc Savage corrected.

She blinked at him. "Mean to say you've been fooling me again?"

"The man who fired the shot and ran was not Mayor Leland Ricketts," Doc Savage said. "He was a man, one of the Roar Devil's men, dressed in clothes exactly like those Mayor Ricketts was wearing."

"How do you know that?"

"Observation," the bronze man told her. "The

man did not run exactly like Mayor Ricketts would have run. And the shooting at D'Aughtell was sour. It was just to get my attention."

"You mean it was a trick?"

"Right. A trick to make us think the Roar Devil was dead."

The girl frowned at him.

"Much as I hate to admit it, you seem to know all, see all. May I compliment you?"

"I made one very bad mistake," Doc told her. "Wouldn't you like to know about that?"

She grinned at him. "I didn't know you ever made mistakes. What was it?"

"In not making sure D'Aughtell had been overcome by the anæsthetic gas here in the office," Doc told her. "He must have seen me break the glass bulb, and held his breath. He was very smooth."

"*Hm-m-m.*" She rubbed her nose thoughtfully. "And this watchman who killed——"

"He did not kill any one," Doc said. "Mayor Ricketts was already dead, his body hidden in the alley. The man I was chasing merely ducked out of sight, while the watchman was shooting into the air."

"Then the watchman is——"

"Due for quite a surprise," Doc Savage told her.

Chapter XVIII

RENDEZVOUS

If the watchman in question had any inkling that he might be headed for a surprise, his deportment gave no sign of it. He was being questioned by the district attorney and his answers were quick and frank.

"How long have you been employed at your present job?" he was asked.

"That's what worried me," the watchman said gloomily. "I just went to work to-day. But look—I got swell references."

The questioning continued, and a policeman came in, saying, "We got a telephone call for a Thomas Ross."

"That's me," said the watchman hastily. "Is it all right for me to go out and talk?"

"Sure," he was told.

The statement was being taken at the factory where Thomas Ross was employed, therefore, he could talk over the telephone with no great fear that the line had been tapped.

"Yeah," he said into the mouthpiece.

"I have it some orders for you," said a rapid voice, which had a trace of an accent.

The watchman recognized it instantly.

"D'Aughtell!" he exploded. "Ain't it kinda risky, you callin' me?"

"That may be, but it is necessary," the voice of the other told him. "It is not so good that things are going. This Doc Savage is maybe smell the rat."

"How do you figure?" The watchman sounded worried. "My end went off all right. He thinks I killed Mayor Ricketts and that Ricketts was the Roar Devil. He ain't got the slightest idea that Ricketts was already dead in that alley before I started shootin'."

"It is not so sure that I am," the other grumbled. "We did it the good job in framing Mayor Ricketts, with guns that we hide in his house, and the note that we fake on his typewriter. But I am not so sure."

"You got orders for me?" asked the watchman abruptly. "I can't stand here gossipin'. The cops may get an itch. You got any orders, D'Aughtell?"

"Orders I have, and plenty of them," said D'Aughtell. "You are to clear out as soon as you can."

"Is that——"

"Maybe not necessary, but the Roar Devil is not take the chance," said the other voice. "You will go to Spring and Metropolitan streets. You know where that is?"

"Sure."

"A guy will be parked in a yellow coupe there. He's one of the big-shot's specials, see, this guy is. The guy is just come up from the city and don't know where the chief is. You take him to the chief. The chief has special work for this guy, and he wants him there in a hurry. You understand it all I am telling?"

"Yeah. What about you, D'Aughtell?"

"Me, you will not see."

The other receiver clicked up.

The watchman finished dictating his statement as if nothing, nothing at all, had happened to interrupt the routine of his first day's work. But at the end of the interview he apparently thought of something, because he began to act nervous. By the time it was over, he was feigning a mild case of the shakes.

"I feel kinda jittery," he told his chief. "This is the first guy I ever killed, and it's kinda got me. How about me takin' the rest of the day off."

He was told that he could have the rest of the day to himself.

"I'm goin' fishin'," the man said. "I think that'll straighten out my nerves better'n anything."

Under the pretense of going fishing, he turned up at the intersection of Spring and Metropolitan. It was a busy corner, with two drug stores, a bank and a department store.

The yellow coupe was parked with a lot of other cars, but it was the only machine of its particular canary hue. The erstwhile watchman walked past it to get a look at the driver.

The driver was worth a second look. At first glance, he seemed near seventy years old, and he might have been mistaken for the proprietor of a medicine show. He had long white hair, a wrinkled and almost paper-white face of considerable area and two enormous ears. He wore a flowing ascot tie, and a large, broad-brimmed black hat.

Altogether he was a picturesque figure. He was smoking an enormous pipe with a white china bowl.

The watchman came over, put foot on the running board and in a tough voice said, "Ain't I seen you before?"

This got a brisk reaction from the old fellow who looked like a medicine show owner. He moved suddenly, and the watchman was looking into the muzzle of a big single-action six-shooter. The hand holding the gun was very white, and had several brown warts on it, but it was steady.

"Nobody but coppers walk up with questions like that," snarled the white-haired one. "I'm waiting for a guy and I ain't gonna be chased off. Get in here and keep your trap shut or I'll blow your head off."

The watchman got into the coupe. Then he laughed.

"I'm Thomas Ross," he said.

"The devil you are?" snarled the other.

"Maybe you was waitin' for me?"

"Maybe I was." The driver yanked his black hat over his eyes, stepped on the starter and the car moved out into traffic. The car sounded as if it were about worn out.

The watchman—Thomas Ross was probably not his real name—studied his companion with great interest. When they had covered half a mile, a strange expression overspread the watchman's face. He grew tense. His hand drifted uneasily for the revolver which he carried.

The old gentleman who looked like a patent medicine faker, asked unexpectedly, "What's got into you?"

"That white hair—it's a wig!" the watchman snarled.

"What of it?" growled the other. "Think I want these rubes to get a gander at my real puss? Shut up, take your hand away from your gun, and tell me where I go. I got hot business with the big one."

The road was really no road at all, but two steep tracks which dodged trees up the steep foot of the giant black stone mountain which was the most prominent feature of the terrain around Powertown. The radiator bubbled and steam spouted around the cap. A carbon knock in the motor sounded as if several men were working on it with small hammers.

"Some chariot," said the watchman, disgustedly.

"Is it much farther?" asked the man with the white hair and big black hat.

"Not much."

The car climbed over a boulder. A tire blew out. The watchman swore, and did not do his share of the work of changing tires. The white-haired man with the appearance of a patent medicine faker, when he got out of the car, seemed unable to straighten. He was a pronounced humpback.

The watchman eyed him curiously. An idea seemed to occur to him.

"Say!" he grunted.

"Yes?" grunted the white-haired one.

"Lot of us ain't never seen the Roar Devil," said the watchman. "Take me, for instance. I don't know 'im by sight. I was just thinkin'."

"Thinkin' what?"

"You might be the Roar Devil yourself."

The other only scowled and jerked the black hat lower. They finished the tire changing in silence, and the little yellow coupe lurched on, groaning, steaming, knocking.

They passed a spot where most of the mountain side had changed position. There had been a slide of considerable importance here. Huge blocks of stone were scattered about. It looked as if the disturbance were recent.

"Landslide?" grunted the man driving.

"No," said the watchman. "That's where the boys set off a dozen quarts of trinitrotoluene—T. N. T. They were hoping to open up Dove Zachies's cache."

"They sure it's in this mountain?" the other queried.

"They're pretty certain. They got two of Dove Zachies's men when this first started, and tortured information out of them. Both said it was this mountain. But they didn't know the exact spot. There was nothin' to do but for us to start blasting, in hopes of opening up the spot. It's a cave, we think."

The coupe jumped another boulder and another tire blew out.

"No more spares," grumbled the driver.

"Devil of a note," said the other. "Well, we can walk. It ain't much farther."

They walked. The white-haired man seemed to have considerable difficulty with his back. He grumbled and complained and had to stop frequently.

They came to what must have been, in years past, a lumber mill. It had gone to ruin. There was one log building which had not fallen down. It seeemed, at first, that the place was deserted, but when they were close, a man came out with a submachine gun.

"Where's everybody?" the watchman asked him.

The man waved an arm. "Up on the hill. They're going to town on this job right now."

"Yeah? How come?"

"They got Dove Zachies," said the man who had been in the decrepit building. "They made him talk. Dove is gonna show where his cache is. Everybody went up to see the excitement."

"Excitement?"

"Yeah." The man with the submachine gun chuckled. "They took all of the prisoners along—you know, them pals of Doc Savage, and the others. They're gonna croak the whole lot together, along with Dove Zachies. Gonna put what T. N. T. we've got left under 'em and blow 'em up. The concussion will probably break that big dam above Powertown, and during the excitement, we'll all clear out. That'll polish the business off."

"A darb of a scheme," said the watchman. "Tell me where the chief went, will you? This guy I got with me is somebody important to the boss. Wants to see him right away."

The other was unsuspicious. He pointed. "Head due north and you'll catch 'em. They ain't been gone long."

The north course proved to be a rocky one. Twice more, they passed great pits in the side of the mountain, spots from which thousands of tons of stone had been pushed by the force of powerful explosive.

"More places where they tried to spot Dove Zachies's cache," said the erstwhile watchman. "We sure done some tall huntin'. But at the same time, we was tryin' to glom onto Zachies."

The humpbacked, white-haired man said nothing. He muttered and sat down frequently to rest, but despite that, they must have traveled faster than those ahead, because they perceived the party before long—a group of fully thirty men, toiling up the precipitous side of the rock-strewn mountain.

The prisoners could be seen, shackled.

Some of the captors were carrying large boxes and being very careful about it. That would be the trinitrotoluene—the T. N. T.

The watchman quickened his pace.

"I'm gonna yell at 'em," he said. "Have 'em wait for us."

He threw back his head. The yell never passed his lips. A strangled gasp did. He slouched forward on his face. The white-haired, humpbacked man had struck him a terrific blow from behind, knocking him senseless.

The man hurriedly jerked off his white wig. Some brisk rubbing removed the wrinkle and dye make-up from his features. He wriggled out of the harness which had lent him the humpbacked aspect.

The gentleman who had resembled a medicine show proprietor became Doc Savage.

Retta Kenn crept up from behind and stopped.

"What a tough ride I had hiding in the back of that coupe," she complained. *"Whew!"*

Chapter XIX

CACHE

Doc Savage produced a hypodermic needle, filled it with a drug which would make the victim unconscious for many hours, and used it on the former watchman.

Retta Kenn said, "I tied into that fellow at the old lumber camp back there. Knocked him out and made him swallow enough sleeping powders to keep him out for a while."

"That was risky," Doc told her. "You might have ruined our plans."

She laughed, and did not seem at all concerned. She appeared, in fact, very happy about the whole thing, enjoying herself hugely.

"This is rich," she said. "This fellow here never even dreamed you were not D'Aughtell when you called. Say, that was a swell job you did of imitating D'Aughtell's voice. But I was afraid he'd see through the make-up. You can't fool a man at close range in broad daylight with make-up."

"He wasn't fooled," Doc told her. "He thought I was wearing the make-up so the yokels up here wouldn't have a description of me."

The girl looked up the mountain. The Roar Devil's party had drawn ahead.

"We'd better step on it," she said.

They "stepped on it," but cautiously, seeking cover, which was not an easy thing to do. They passed another spot where blasting had been done in search for Dove Zachies's cache. The party ahead filed into a ravine. They managed to distinguish D'Aughtell in the cavalcade.

Speaking as if she knew it were a fact but just wanted to repeat it to convince herself, the girl said, "You left Dove Zachies and his men behind, knowing D'Aughtell would tip his pals off to where they are so they could be carried off. You did that deliberately, so that the Roar Devil would find Dove Zachies's cache."

"That is past history," Doc Savage told her. "You might be a little more careful. After all, if they discover us now, things will be in a bad jam."

She was a little more attentive to caution. They entered a patch of boulders and scrambled forward hurriedly—so hurriedly that they all but gave themselves away, for the Roar Devil's cavalcade had stopped.

"Stay here," Doc told the girl.

She plainly did not like that, but she said, "All right."

"And I mean stay here!" he added grimly. "No matter *what* happens!"

"I'll stay," she snapped. "But I can take care of myself, and don't you——"

Doc left her bragging about her own abilities, and went on. There was the silence of a ghost in his going, and instead of shoving up his head, he used a small periscopic affair of a slender tube and mirrors to survey the terrain ahead.

He came to a point where he could hear his quarry talking, but did not dare show himself enough to take a look at them.

Dove Zachies was wailing, "Now listen, a long time ago you guys offered me a deal——"

"Where is the cache?" a harsh, singsong voice ripped.

That was the Roar Devil's voice.

Doc Savage took a chance and lifted his head for a look. He was unfortunate. The Roar Devil was not in sight, but fully twenty others were, and any instant they might see the bronze man. He lowered his head and contented himself with listening.

"Now look," Dove Zachies gulped desperately. "I'll throw in with you, see? I'll even take a mighty small split. You can use my dope—the stuff in my cache—to whip your organization into shape and start operations. And I'll play along with you, and not——"

"All right," said the singing voice. "Show us the cache!"

"You'll play ball——"

"We will."

"Gee, thanks!" gasped Zachies. "Now, look. The cache is right here, see? You stamp on this cracked piece of rock and the whole thing hinges up——"

There was a stamping noise, then a grinding of stone. Several men swore or muttered. The secret door must have opened.

"And to think we dang near blasted this mountain apart huntin' this spot," a man laughed.

Doc Savage chanced another look, but could make out nothing. He listened. Sounds indicated the men were filing down into a subterranean passage of some description.

Doc Savage waited until silence fell. Then he lifted his head. No one in sight, but he could not see the mouth of the cave, if that was what it was. He crept forward.

There was a cleverly constructed trapdoor affair in the stone side of the ravine, and this was open. Two men, holding automatic rifles, stood on guard outside. They were not doing a very good job of guarding. Their attention was riveted upon what was going on underground. They were bending forward, listening.

Doc Savage fished out one of the little glass bulbs which he used so conveniently. He tossed it. Both of the men heard the sound it made behind them—as if a bird's egg had been dropped. They turned. Then they went to sleep and fell over.

The bronze man stripped off his shoes and went down the side of the ravine. He paused a moment at the mouth of the cave. It seemed to slope upward. Voice rumbles came from deep within the cave.

It was a nice place for a secret door. No doubt, every rain sent a flood of water down the ravine, and that would wash away many marks left by users of the place.

Doc Savage went in. The floor slanted sharply. Then there were steps.

The first dozen steps were wide, comfortable. The next few were narrow, as if in the building of the place, the excavator had gotten tired or changed his mind. The alteration in the width of the steps nearly caused the bronze man to make a noise. He went on.

There was a room. Flashlights illuminated it. It was arched and like a vault, entirely of stone.

Several men were holding another up on their shoulders. The top man was Dove Zachies. He was working with a hammer and a cold chisel, cutting into concrete that had been dyed to make it look like the native rock.

"Pretty slick, wasn't it?" he was saying. "Even if you had opened up this cave with your blasting, I doubt if you would have found the lock boxes with the documents in them."

He perspired, and his hammer clanged and rock fragments clattered down on the heads of those below.

"I guess I oughta listened to reason at the first," Zachies said. "But you see, I been gathering this stuff for years. It's cost me no telling how much money! There is nothing else like it any where. With this stuff, I can do darn near what I want, and make a lot of other people do it, too. I didn't want to give it up."

His cold chisel slipped out of his hand and flew across the room. Some one found it and brought it back, requesting him, profanely to be careful.

Doc Savage shifted position slightly. He was looking for the mastermind, the person who had been designated as the Roar Devil. He did not see him.

Monk, Ham and the other prisoners stood along one wall, each with handcuffs on his wrists.

Dove Zachies beat the cold chisel steadily with the hammer. He seemed worried, almost terrified, and he talked in a wild, hurried voice. Possibly, it relieved his mind in some manner.

"I first got the idea of gettin' this stuff together more'n ten years ago," he said. "That was when a bird in my mob made a death-bed statement about a judge who had killed a man in a fight and nobody ever suspected. You can bet that judge was very good to me after that."

The hammer banged. Concrete bits sprayed out, even to as far as where Doc Savage crouched, just outside the room.

"Most of the stuff is genuine evidence on somebody," Dove Zachies went on. "Some of it has been framed. But the victims don't know that."

"Hurry up," some one said.

"Getting to it," Zachies chuckled wildly. "Now you take my dope on the lad who's slated for mayor. He's an up-and-coming young politician and people think he's straight. They think he doesn't show favor to anybody. That's true—except for me. That lad will do anything I say, just about, because in this lock box I'm digging out of the ceiling here, I've got proof that his sister killed a guy.

"The killing was a frame-up, but the sister and nobody else knows that. Take that paper alone. It's worth half a million to the right guy, easy. Sure it is! It's just like having the key to the city. And there's plenty of more like it in this box!"

He gave a few more ordinarily lusty blows with the hammer. The cold chisel made sounds of hitting metal.

"We're all gonna go places with this stuff," Dove Zachies said expansively, to those below him. "The Roar Devil has drawn you birds together in one of the biggest and best mobs ever organized! With this stuff I've got in my tin boxes here, we can take over the whole eastern part of the United States."

He had enlarged the hole above him. He inserted the chisel and wrenched. A metal box came out. It was a tin container of the type commonly used to hold documents. He passed it down, continued prying, and five more of the metal boxes came out.

"I've got the keys," he said.

They lowered him. The men crowded in a compact group, except for those watching the prisoners. Doc Savage took a chance and stared into the room, even shoving his head and shoulders inside. He could not see the Roar Devil. The man was hidden by his followers.

Sounds indicated the boxes were being opened. Then documents crackled. There were grunts of satisfaction.

"I could peddle this stuff to professional blackmailers for a million bucks, easy!" Dove Zachies said loudly. "It's taken me years and thousands and thousands of dollars to assemble that stuff."

A man said, "Shall we shoot Zachies now?"

Zachies must have looked at the Roar Devil's face.

"You—you're gonna double-cross me!" he screamed.

There was a scuffle, short and ferocious. Dove Zachies screamed all during the struggle, his voice a frenzied bleating remindful of a rabbit caught by dogs. Then they tossed him out with the other prisoners. He could not stand, his legs shook so, and he sagged down on the floor and began to blubber and sob in horror.

Then the singsong voice of the Roar Devil began to speak.

"These documents are all that I wanted," he said. "They are, as Zachies says, invaluable. There is blackmail evidence of every kind here. It is all on wealthy men and men high in public office. With it, we can get for ourselves all kinds of privileges. These papers are the one link necessary to complete my organization."

He apparently riffled through more of the papers. But he was still behind the jam of men in the room, and Doc Savage could not see him.

"Wonderful!" the Roar Devil resumed. "Here is

evidence that would hang several of our best-known criminals. I have tried to get these men to join me, and they have refused. They will change their minds, now."

On the floor, Dove Zachies bubbled, "You can't kill me! You can't! You told me——"

"Shut up!" he was told.

"Yes, do be a man," the Roar Devil suggested. "Of course, you should have known you would not be turned free, no more than the others, those men of Doc Savage's."

"Whatcha gonna do with me?" Zachies gasped.

"As you know, we brought along some hundreds of pounds of T. N. T.," Zachies was told. "The plan was to set off a blast which would not only wipe out Doc Savage's aides, but destroy their bodies. That still seems an excellent scheme. We'll let you keep them company, Zachies."

At that point, one of the prisoners spoke up. It was the gaunt geologist, Johnny.

"Another explosion of consequence will cause a slippage of the earth along a subterranean fault line," he said. "That big dam above Powertown will undoubtedly collapse. It is under considerable strain now, although not in immediate danger of giving way. I suggest that you dispose of us, if you are going to insist on that, in a manner which will not menace other lives."

Johnny spoke calmly enough that only one who knew him well could tell that he was probably scared as he had ever been in his not uneventful, life.

"It is probable that Doc Savage will have the police watching the roads for known criminals," the Roar Devil singsonged. "Doc Savage thinks Mayor Leland Ricketts, who is now dead, was the Roar Devil. He will naturally expect my organization to disband. And he will have the police watching. But we could easily get away in the excitement which would follow a dam break. You see, we have merely to switch on my apparatus which so completely eliminates all sound, and——"

There was a loud clatter and a stifled cry down the passage behind Doc Savage. The Roar Devil had not been speaking loudly. This new noise was as disturbing as the explosion of dynamite.

Chapter XX

HELL IN A ROCK BOX

A man pitched into the passage from the room. It happened with shocking abruptness. The fellow had not been with the others, but had stood just inside, and Doc Savage, thanks to the tableau in the center of the stone chamber, had been unaware of the man's presence.

The man slammed headlong into Doc Savage. Doc struck him. The fellow was driven backward. But he was a big man and strong, and he had gotten a grip on the bronze man's coat. He kept the grip.

The coat came apart in the middle of the back and was torn completely off the bronze giant, except for the sleeves. The man who had been struck carried it with him as he tumbled away.

Losing the coat was little short of a disaster. In the pockets reposed the anæsthetic bombs with which the bronze man had been intending to overcome those in the stone room. He lunged for the coat.

The man with the coat apparently realized he had a prize. He was still on his feet. He ran with the coat.

Men charged for Doc. A gun blasted. Its report all but split eardrums. Doc was weaving, and the slug missed him.

Monk howled. Renny roared. Both pitched into the fight, although their wrists were handcuffed. Ham and Johnny also mixed in the fight. They were joined by Dove Zachies and his captured crew, fighting for their lives.

The next instant, the stone cell was a bawling, screaming bedlam. Forty men fought in a space hardly more than that many feet in each direction.

Guns banged. Lead made ugly sounds in flesh. Powder fumes smarted throats.

The singsong voice of the Roar Devil lashed out.

"The T. N. T.!" he shrilled. "No shooting! A bullet might hit it!"

Every one heard him. It was a thought that chilled spines. Somewhere in the room, the boxes of explosive had been stacked. Not another shot was fired. And men began to be very careful that they did not hit anything but other men when they swung blows.

It dawned on Monk that there was going to be no more gunplay.

"*Whee!*" he squawled. "For years, I've looked for a fight like this!"

Doc Savage found a round, hard skull. He slipped his hands down to the back of the neck. An instant before he tightened his fingers, the victim emitted a howl and Doc knew it was D'Aughtell.

Doc did something to the back of D'Aughtell's neck—something it would have taken one skilled in chiropractic and surgery to explain, something that induced a nerve paralysis that rendered most of the man's body temporarily useless. The bronze man had practiced that for years. He could do it with a squeeze and a twist, and get results that smacked of the touch of a genius.

Three men tried for the door in a fighting wedge. They did not make it. One was driven aside, so that he bumped his senses out against the wall. One was knocked out neatly and simply. The other ran the other way, after having his right arm nearly jerked from its socket.

Monk was still yelling, a great, joyful senseless bawling. He always did that when he fought. He went completely haywire—and had the time of his life.

Only a sporadic rumble came from Renny. But the awful impact of his great fists was a sound that could be picked out above all the rest. Johnny managed to fight in comparative dignity.

"I'll be superamalgamated!" he said once, when something untoward happened to him.

Over on the other side of the room, Ham swore a few educated vituperatives and wished mildly that he had his sword cane.

Doc Savage, sidling along the wall, fell over something. The something squealed. It was the pig, Habeas Corpus, in a gunny sack. Some one had brought him along.

Doc untied the sack and shook Habeas out to add to the general uproar.

The fray, to the death though it was, had its comical aspects. Monk started it off. He hit Renny by mistake, and was knocked down for his pains. After that, Monk grabbed a figure in the intense darkness, asked, "Who is it?" and reacted according to the answer he got.

Occasionally, flashlights came on. But they always went out quickly, because the light was certain to draw a rush of enemies.

The Roar Devil was first to lose his nerve.

"Get out!" he shrilled. "Let them follow you outside where we can use our guns!"

Doc Savage made straight for the sound of the voice. He spread his arms wide, and he made no noise at all. Sure enough, he encountered his quarry. He took a terrific blow in the midriff, a blow that was like the sound of a hard-swung ax against wood.

Doc chopped with a fist. The blow landed but glancingly, only driving the other back. The Roar Devil was moaning. He had hurt his fist, broken bones in it, with that first blow.

Doc hit him again, very hard, just as the man fired a gun. The fellow's fear of personal injury had overcome his fear of hitting the T. N. T. The slug started the bronze man's shoulder smarting, and he hit again with his fist. That one landed squarely.

The next instant, a slack body was in his arms. The Roar Devil had been knocked back against the stone side of the chamber and had bounced, senseless. Doc held him long enough to be sure that he still breathed. Then he let the fellow down on the floor.

Men were escaping through the passage. They were not having an easy time of it, but they were getting away, one at a time, and as they escaped, the uproar became proportionately less.

Finally, only two men were fighting. They battled viciously, and in silence. Then one of them landed a particularly hard blow.

"Ouch!" roared Monk.

"You ugly ape!" gritted the second combatant.

"Ham!" Monk squawled. "Was that you I've been fightin' the last five minutes?"

Ham said something blistering. "Why'd you stop yelling, you accident of nature? How was I to know that it was you?"

"I got hoarse," Monk snarled. "Why didn't you say something? Say, I gotta notion to paste you!"

Doc Savage found a flashlight and thumbed it on. He roved the beam. His four aides were on their feet. So was Dove Zachies and three of his gang.

Monk ceased glaring at Ham, looked about on the floor, found a submachine gun which some one had dropped, and managed to pick it up with his manacled hands. He maneuvered it into a position where he could fire it, and started for the door.

"Wait!" Doc said sharply.

"I'm goin' out," Monk growled. "Them guys ain't gonna get away!"

"They'll be watching the entrance," Doc told him. "They'll shoot you down as you go out."

Monk stopped. "Yeah, they might, at that."

A sharp, ugly roar of shots came to their ears. The firing was outside, a machine gun.

"One of them limbering up his gun," Renny boomed uneasily. "Say, we're in a jam! We can't go near that entrance. They'll hear us and turn loose. There ain't no shelter in that passage."

"And no doubt they will hold us in here until they can get explosives," Ham said ominously. "A grenade or two tossed inside will just about finish us."

Doc Savage found two more flashlights. He held them all together, so that they made a bright bundle of light, and began going over the subterranean room. He found the boxes of T. N. T., miraculously undisturbed in the fighting, but passed it up for a pair of large cases, fitted with carrying straps, which stood near by. He bent over these.

Monk ambled over. "What's that? You think it'll help us?"

"It should," Doc told him.

"What is it?"

"An apparatus for producing sonic waves of a somewhat peculiar nature on an ultra-short wave length," Doc told him.

Monk knew something of the science of sound. He looked interested, said, "Yeah?"

Doc Savage had gotten the cases over. They seemed to hook together with a flexible conductor. There was a lid on each box. He removed them and began pouring light over the intricate mechanism within.

"Not as complicated as might be expected," he said. "This one, of course, only works over a short distance. They must have another, a larger one, which they used when setting off the blasts."

"Yeah, I heard 'em say they did have," Monk replied. "How does that trap work?"

"Ultra-short sound waves can do queer things," Doc said. "For instance, did you ever see certain insects exposed to sonic vibrations set up by the contraction and expansion of a quartz crystal as a high frequency alternating current is passed through it?"

"Long Tom monkeys with that stuff," Monk said. "I think he told me one time that it would kill the bugs, sometimes."

"Exactly," Doc said, working over the mechanism. "Ultra-short sonic waves result in rather unusual phenomena. Scientists, as a matter of fact, do not know all that is to be known about them, by a good deal."

"Which adds up to what in this case?" Monk persisted.

The machine gun stuttered again outside. They did not, however, hear any bullets enter the passage.

"This device," Doc indicated the boxes, "makes sonic waves on some infinitely short wave length. Those waves seem to have the quite peculiar property of——"

"Stopping all sound!" Monk finished.

"No," Doc told him, "that is hardly possible. The sonic waves simply paralyze the drum of the human ear until it is not susceptible to sound. The sonic waves, the air vibration, does something to the ear mechanism that renders it incapable of registering sound."

Monk grunted explosively.

"Is that the secret of the periods of absolute silence?" he demanded.

"It is."

Doc Savage worked over the apparatus. He had put the connections together in the most obvious places. Now he began turning switches. The results were deafening.

The cavern was filled with a tremendous, ear-splitting roar. The sound seemed everywhere; it made their heads ache with its power. It was a sound such as nothing conceivable might make.

Doc turned the switches off. The roar died.

"That explains something which was puzzling me," he said. "That roaring noise!"

"What makes it?" Monk demanded.

"This apparatus, when it is not adjusted properly," Doc told him.

Renny boomed, "So that mystery is cleared up! Boy, I heard that roar a time or two, and it sure had me buffaloed!"

Doc Savage scrutinized the instrument closely, obviously trying to fathom its secrets.

"It requires very close adjustment," he decided

aloud. "A thing of this kind naturally would. It is amazingly complicated."

He continued his tinkering.

Monk pointed at the apparatus. "What are you going to do, if you can make it work?"

"Turn it on," Doc said. "It will be of some help in getting close to the mouth of that passage. They cannot hear us coming. We may be able to pick some of them off, then rush them."

So unexpectedly that it surprised them all vastly, a feminine voice sounded.

"Say," demanded Retta Kenn from outside, "isn't anybody left alive in there?"

Doc Savage deserted the silence-making machine and ran through the passage.

Retta Kenn was in the bright sunlight outside. She held a submachine gun, with which she menaced a cluster of cowed Roar Devil gunmen.

"I made them line up as they came out," she said happily. "I got this gun from one of the guards you overcame outside the cave mouth."

Doc Savage stared at her. He did not say anything. He looked as if he would have liked to say something.

"I'm good," Retta Kenn said. "You'll have to admit it."

Her face was a wreck. Most of the skin was gone from her nose and the end of her chin. Her face was also dirty.

"I told you not to follow me," Doc said.

"It's a good thing I did." She waved at her prisoners. "These would have gotten away."

"You followed me," Doc told her. "You fell down those steps inside, and touched off the excitement before I was ready for it. Otherwise, I could have gotten them all with that anæsthetic gas, and there would not have been any danger to anybody."

She grinned at him impishly. "You know everything, don't you?"

Doc Savage said nothing. He began searching

the prisoners and disarming such of them as had
weapons. On one, he found the keys to the handcuffs
which secured his men, and he turned them loose.
They transferred the handcuffs to the more belliger-
ent of their prisoners.

Monk blew on his wrists vigorously when the
handcuffs were off. During the fight, the bracelets
had scraped most of the skin and some of the flesh
from his hairy wrist.

He glowered at the captives, and said, "I gotta
notion to go right down the line and knock 'em all
stiff!"

The prisoners squirmed. They apparently thought
he meant it.

"I know what I'll do," Monk decided. "I'll get that
Roar Devil and tie him up. We don't want him to
get away."

He stalked into the cave with a flashlight.

Retta Kenn looked at Doc Savage. "Have you got
enough evidence on these men to get them what they
deserve in a court of law? They all should be hung."

"They will never see a court of law," Doc Savage
said.

"What do you mean?" she demanded.

Doc Savage did not give her the satisfaction of
knowing that all of the prisoners would be consigned
to the "crime college" which he maintained farther
upstate.

The girl did not need to know about the "college."
Few individuals outside Doc Savage and his group of
five men did know of the existence of the place.

Monk came out of the cave, triumphantly dragging a limp figure.

"Here he is!" he grinned, and tossed the Roar
Devil on the ground.

Retta Kenn stared at the unconscious Roar Devil.

"Why," she gasped, "it's my boss, V. Venable
Mear!"

Doc Savage went back into the cave, partially to
make sure none of the unconscious men there came to

their senses and tried to make a break, and partially to get away from Retta Kenn.

She was a very capable young woman. She had as much nerve as any member of the feminine sex he had ever encountered. Sometimes he believed she had too much nerve. At times she was braver than any one with good sense should be.

And she irritated him.

None of the fight victims seemed about to awaken, so Doc Savage devoted attention to the sonic transmitter which had caused so much mystery.

It was an interesting device, something well ahead of current scientific discoveries. He resolved to take it to his skyscraper laboratory and ascertain fully the principles upon which it had worked. D'Aughtell, no doubt, had invented it, and D'Aughtell, with the proper persuasion, would tell all about it.

The apparatus should prove an interesting study. And it, or some adaptation of it, might prove useful in the future. Doc would work hard at it.

He was mistaken. He would work hard, but not at this. For there was another mystery that would occupy his attention. A mystery deeper than this, carrying with it peril and death in fantastic forms; a mystery chronicled in the history of the ancient Vikings, but written there in such a manner that, down through the ages, no man had dreamed its amazing significance. Unknown through history, because men had forgotten the meaning of one word, Qui.

The *Quest of Qui* was to take Doc Savage into the bleak fastnesses of Labrador, and to an island which held a thing so fantastic that the world could not comprehend. Qui was there, and the horror of Qui, the mystery of Qui, was to afford the bronze man and his aides adventure more perilous, danger more hideous, than they had ever before encountered.

But Doc Savage, blissfully unaware of what was to come, left the sonic apparatus after a while and went out into the sunlight.

Monk had Retta Kenn to one side. He had apparently been telling her things about Doc.

"He's quite a guy," she said. "He'd make a swell husband for a gal who likes excitement."

"Doc's not interested in women," Monk said. "But how about *me* for a husband?"

"Heaven forbid!" the girl said fervently.

DOC SAVAGE

To the world at large, Doc Savage is a strange, mysterious figure of glistening bronze skin and golden eyes. To his fans he is the greatest adventure hero of all time, whose fantastic exploits are unequaled for hair-raising thrills, breathtaking escapes, blood-curdling excitement!

☐	THE EVIL GNOME	2134	$1.25
☐	THE MOUNTAIN MONSTER	2239	$1.25
☐	THE MAN OF BRONZE	6352	$1.25
☐	THE STONE MAN	6419	$1.25
☐	THE BOSS OF TERROR	6424	$1.25
☐	THE THOUSAND HEADED MAN	6471	$1.25
☐	THE RED TERRORS	6486	$1.25
☐	DOC SAVAGE: HIS APOCALYPTIC LIFE	8834	$1.25
☐	THE KING MAKER	10042	$1.25
☐	THE PHANTOM CITY	10119	$1.25
☐	THE MYSTIC MULLAH	10120	$1.25
☐	FEAR CAY	10121	$1.25
☐	LAND OF ALWAYS NIGHT	10122	$1.25
☐	FANTASTIC ISLAND	10125	$1.25
☐	QUEST OF QUI	10126	$1.25

Buy them at your local bookstore or use this handy coupon for ordering:

Bantam Books, Inc., Dept. DS, 414 East Golf Road, Des Plaines, Ill. 60016

Please send me the books I have checked above. I am enclosing $_____ (please add 35¢ to cover postage and handling). Send check or money order —no cash or C.O.D.'s please.

Mr/Mrs/Miss_____

Address_____

City_____State/Zip_____

DS—5/77

Please allow three weeks for delivery. This offer expires 5/78.